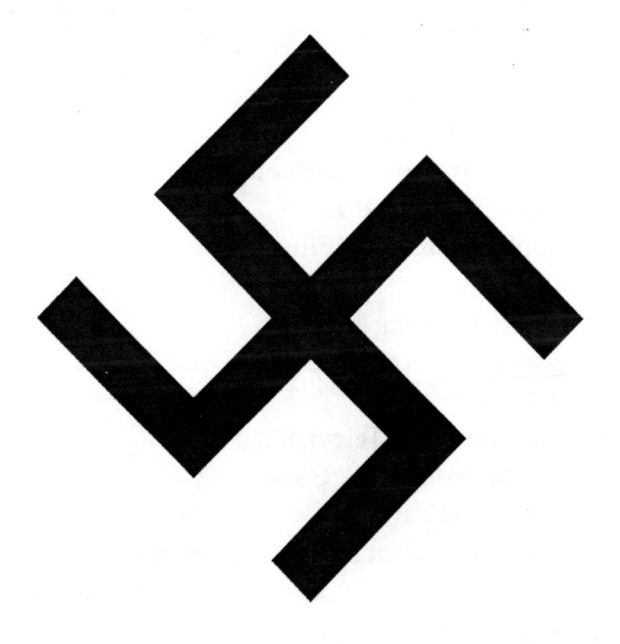

Adolf in
WONDERLAND

Also by CARLTON MELLICK III

Satan Burger
Electric Jesus Corpse
Sunset With a Beard (stories)
Razor Wire Pubic Hair
Teeth and Tongue Landscape
The Steel Breakfast Era
The Baby Jesus Butt Plug
Fishy-fleshed
The Menstruating Mall
Ocean of Lard (with Kevin L. Donihe)
Punk Land
Sex and Death in Television Town
Sea of the Patchwork Cats
The Haunted Vagina
Cancer-cute (Avant Punk Army Exclusive)
War Slut
Sausagey Santa
Ugly Heaven, Beautiful Hell (with Jeffrey Thomas)

Adolf in WONDERLAND

CARLTON MELLICK III

AVANT PUNK

AVANT PUNK BOOKS

AN IMPRINT OF ERASERHEAD PRESS

ERASERHEAD PRESS
205 NE BRYANT
PORTLAND, OR 97211

WWW.ERASERHEADPRESS.COM

ISBN: 1-933929-61-8

Copyright © 2007 by Carlton Mellick III
www.avantpunk.com
Cover art copyright © 2007 by Jeff Powers
ravenofsorrows.deviantart.com

All rights reserved. No part of this book may be reproduced or transmitted in any form or by any means, electronic or mechanical, including photocopying, recording, or by any information storage and retrieval system, without the written consent of the publisher, except where permitted by law.

Printed in the USA.

AUTHOR NOTE

I have always had an interest in Nazi Germany for some reason. Perhaps it is because of my heritage; I am a descendent of both German Nazis and German Jews. I once had a girlfriend who thought it was kind of romantic that my mother's bloodline was responsible for exterminating much of my father's bloodline. Of course, I don't think that's exactly how it happened. I don't really know much about that part of my family history. A lot of that history has been lost, much of it on purpose.

My grandfather, born Carlton Von Opperman, was luckily not in Germany during the holocaust, as he was adopted into the Mellick family in America prior to WW2. We assume that my great grandfather and his family were not so lucky, as they were never heard from again.

My mother, Elke Beetz-Wittenborn, was born in Germany and came to this country when she was a kid in the early '50s. Because Germans were still very unpopular in the US in the early '50s, they were met with a lot of prejudice, especially my mother who was tormented and constantly abused by her school teachers (encouraging her classmates to do the same). Her family beared an incredible guilt for being German and completely denied much of their heritage, so I don't really know much about my German ancestry. There were rumors that the Wittenborn side saved a family of Jews by hiding them in their attic. There were rumors that there was a gestapo agent on the

Beetz side of my family, as well as several Nazi supporters. I'll never know the truth, though.

My interest in Nazi Germany gave me the urge to write a book about the Nazi utopia. But instead of setting the book within the Nazi utopia, I decided to take utopian Nazis and send them on a quest into a surreal world, such as Wonderland. Wonderland represents chaos, randomness, disorder, the out-of-control, the imperfect. The Nazi utopia is the opposite of this. It represents efficiency, purity, order, control, perfection. These are two worlds that are destined to collide, which is what happens when Adolf goes to Wonderland.

Young Adolf Hitler (as this book was originally titled) took me eight years to complete. Aside from the eleven novels I abandoned pre-Electric Jesus Corpse, Young Adolf Hitler was the fourth book I started and the twentieth to be finished. (The third book still has yet to be finished.)

Perfectionism is the thing that slowed down the writing process for this book, which is pretty ironic considering the point of the story.

- Carlton Mellick III

Contents

PART ONE: Chasing the White Rabbit

    Blood Red Sky ... 11
    Mr. Bartender ... 17
    Mr. Wheel ... 23
    Mr. Sausage ... 30
    Mr. Nothing ... 36
    Mr. Eyebrows ... 41
    Mrs. Ghost ... 45
    Mr. Wheel ... 47
    Mrs. Perfect ... 53
    Mr. D ... 57

PART TWO: Down the Rabbit Hole

    Mr. Small ... 61
    Mr. Handlebar Mustache ... 65
    Mrs. Darkness ... 71
    Mr. Noseless ... 75
    Mr. Roger Eyebrows ... 81
    Mr. Song ... 85
    Mr. Bartender ... 89
    Mrs. Neat ... 95
    Father Noseless ... 102
    Mrs. Pig ... 110

PART THREE: The Queen of Eels

    Mr. and Mrs. Hitler . . . 115
    Mrs. Mantimeleon . . . 117
    Mrs. Stick and Mr. Mohawk . . . 120
    Mr. Warthog . . . 123
    Mr. Partner . . . 127
    Mr. Conjoined . . . 132
    Mr. Hitlerhog . . . 137
    Mr. Eel . . . 141
    Mrs. Eel . . . 145
    Mr. Master Race . . . 150
    Mr. Imperfect . . . 158

PART ONE
Chasing the White Rabbit

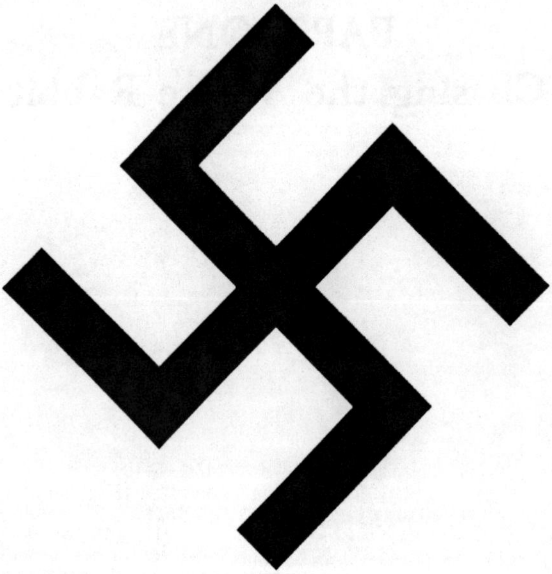

Blood Red Sky

The color red was infesting the landscape, red suffocating the yellow out of the sun overhead:

Two nearly identical looking men were dragging their bodies through the desert. They could feel the sour HOT liquefy their skin under their uniforms, crying from their pores, steam crawling up like goblin spiders, choke-tight collars, blood vessels popping from the surface of their necks to breathe. They were sweating on the inside as well as out. The salty ooze drizzled from their necks down their sleeves to the white bands around their upper left arms, making their swastikas a darker shade of red, as bloody as the sky.

"It should be just over the next hill," the older one told the younger one, gawking at him with tangy eyes.

"You said that the last hill, and the hill before that," said the younger one, noticing that dirt from the wind had coated his partner's blond hair, giving it a brownish tint that he found utterly disgusting and disgraceful.

"What are you suggesting with that?" asked the older man with a furrowed brow.

The younger one did not answer, shifting his head

to watch a swarm of millipedes flying in the distance. *Incompetent old fool*, he said in his mind.

They had been dropped off by train in the middle of oblivion. At the train station they found themselves alone, the only passengers to leave the train, looking at each other and at the barren landscape and back at each other as the train pulled away.

The station had long been abandoned. It consisted of four buildings, each with two doors, four walls, but no roof or floor. The buildings were infested with thorny weeds and tractor tire mountains draped in crumbly flowers of purple-pink paint.

They were instructed to follow the road west, but there weren't any roads. Nor were there any signs hanging around to tell them where they were or where they could go. It was like they were the first passengers to get off at that stop for over a hundred years.

There was, however, a slight snake trail that might have once been a path. So they followed it west, to the hills in the distance, where they hoped they might find the town that they are looking for.

"It has been five miles," said the younger man, his eyes went from sea-blue to sun-red.

As they were climbing the hill, the sun drip-dripped its blood onto the horizon as sweat drip-dripped into their eyes to sting and blind.

"It only *seems* like five miles because of the heat," said the older man. "It has probably only been one, *two* max."

They pondered this: *Five miles? No, it could not have been that many. When did we leave the train sta-*

tion? It was morning. The sun was in the east. Now it is in the west. Have we been walking all day? The heat is playing games. We must have gotten to the train station later than noon and did not realize it. It has only been an hour . . . two hours . . .

The swarm of millipedes were still crispy-buzzing, flying like a tornado in the distance. Maybe they were scorpion-flies. Maybe some of them had landed behind their necks and injected poison into their brains so that their thoughts would not flow smoothly.

At the top of the hill, they found another stretch of desert, all the way to mountains in the distance. Here there were purple bushes and cacti that seemed to be carved from steel. The sky reflecting off the sand appeared flaming red, like a Martian landscape. No sign of any town or any living creature. Silent like a painting.

"There is no town out here," the younger man said, smug-nasty face thrown in his superior's direction.

"It is here somewhere. We just need to find it."

The young man didn't seem as optimistic. His smug face returned, shaking his head, not bothering to respond. He wanted his superior to be wrong. He wanted to notify the bureau of his inefficiency, so that the older man would be executed and the younger man would be promoted to his position.

Officers of the SS were always exterminated by firing squad rather than injection, because it's a more honorable way to die. They were allowed their closest friends and associates to do the shooting, all lined up in front of them. If the younger man got his way, he would be a part of the older man's firing squad. It would have been so satisfying for him to put a bullet in his superior's brain.

"If the town was not in the middle of nowhere," the older officer explained, "he would not be hiding there."

"Completely cut off from the rest of the world..." the young officer said to himself, stampeding down the hill.

"Yes, the people here are *free* to do whatever they want."

"Impossible," the young man shouted. "That is illegal."

The older man agreed. "It is *heinously* illegal."

"Then why has not anyone put a stop to it?"

"Do not ask me." The older man shrugged, worn-ragged shoulders. "Ask the Fuhrer."

The young one whipped his head back to the trail and continued, "How is our society to reach ultimate *perfection* when whole towns are slipping under nose?"

"It is only one town," said the superior officer. "An entire world of consistency will bury this town of randomness in time. Let evolution take care of eliminating the weak as it was designed to do."

"It is still a disgusting thought."

They stagger-walked the trail halfway to the mountains, stiff-legged from the either hour-long or day-long hike. A heavy wind emptied in from between the hills, rivering through their dusty blond hair. Dirt crunched between the younger man's eyelids when he squeezed them shut. He raised his briefcase to his face to block the wind.

They got to the end of the snake trail. The younger man stopped to blink sand out of his eyes until he could see the distance more clearly.

"What is that?" the younger officer asked, pointing at something far away.

The older man brushed the wind out of his face and looked carefully. Then he saw it:

A town.

They walked across the desert until they reached its edge.

It wasn't a *real* town. It was like what a doll would consider a town. It was about as high as their waists, maybe thirty feet wide and fifty feet long.

"What do you think it is?" the younger man asked, stepping inside the miniature town, crunch-walking the gray foam street. A row of cardboard buildings was beside him, spray-painted white, red, tan.

"It is some kind of model," the older one said, waiting by the edge. "Maybe a replica of the town we are looking for."

The younger officer seemed to be disappointed, even though this model was proof that a civilization was nearby.

"One of the town's children must have made it," he said.

"Excellent craftsmanship for a child."

The younger man shook his head. "It is appalling." He took a few more steps down the little road, crushing the foam board, toppling the trees along the sidewalk.

"The town must be very close," the older man said.

The younger officer knelt to a miniature tavern in the center of the town and peeked his monster eye within. It was blank, white. Lacking furniture, a bar, a bartender. He said, "The child did not care much for detail."

The younger man turned back to his superior officer, but he was not there.

"Where..." he called.

Silence.

Twitching, his sightballs scanned the terrain, but the older officer was nowhere in sight. At first, he thought maybe his partner just abandoned the awkward situation— two important officers lost in the desert was definitely a situation worth abandoning. But the older man could not have possibly run fast enough to escape his vision. Nor was there a suitable place for him to hide. The older man was just *gone*, vanished off the face of the planet.

The SS officer left the model to look for his partner, eyes wandering across the red desert, refusing the concept of an unexplainable disappearance.

"This is absurd," he said to himself. "He has to be here somewhere," standing pathetic next to a toy neighborhood, as the dirty wind returned from the hills.

Mr. Bartender

The youngish man awoke in someplace new.

Someplace dark. His head was hammering pressure out through the eyeballs — a hangover headache as if the night before had been filled with many-many rounds of heavy hard drinking. A thick bitterness in his mouth, insect-bitter. Sliding his rough tongue against the carpet-textured roof of his mouth made him gag.

His eyes opened to his hands as his hands opened to a wooden table. Looking beyond the gritty fingers, he noticed a piss beer stain down his chest. His uniform was soiled, wrinkled, and soggy. The swastika on his shoulder looked faded behind a layer of dust. He didn't know why his uniform was in such a condition. He didn't know where he was or how long he had been there.

He looked up. He was in a bar. A bartender was staring at him from behind the counter. The bartender's look was . . . hollow. Stiff and stale. His expressions were that of a paper doll.

There was no one else. Just a bartender. He didn't move, standing there like a marionette made from balls of newspaper.

"How did I get here?" the youngish man asked the bartender, slurring words. He was considerably drunk.

The bartender did not answer.

"How long have I been here?"

The bartender shook his head in response but did not say words.

"Is this ___ Town?" asked the youngish man.

Another expressionless face as response.

The youngish man turned around on his creaky stool. The room was as blank as the bartender. A few tables. No people.

"Where is everyone?"

He got off the stool to notice that he was very dizzy. He had a blood-soaked brain and his walk was bobbly like clay.

"Asleep," said the bartender, causing his customer to jerk in surprise to hear him speak. The bartender's voice as stiff as his look. "Everyone's asleep at this time."

Clenching his forehead, the youngish man tried to remember what he was doing there. The intoxication had broken the memory section of his brain.

He thought to himself: *I must be in ___ Town, yes I know that is where I am supposed to be, I am on a mission to, to find someone, kill someone? or bring him somewhere... but who?*

"Adolf?" asked the bartender, his voice paralyzing with its emptiness. "Another drink?"

The youngish man shook his starry head, still trying to make logic. Then he thought, *wait a minute...*

"Adolf?" he asked the bartender, fuming words at him. "Did you just call me *Adolf?*"

The bartender nodded his cardboard head. "Is it not your name . . . Adolf Hitler?"

"No, I am . . ."

Long pause. He bit his tongue, dig-scooping through the flesh-drawers of his brain for answers.

"Look," said the bartender, pointing over the counter. "It says it right here, on your uniform."

They looked at a patch on his uniform and read the words:

> . . . Praise God
> . . . Praise the Nation
> . . . Praise *Adolf Hitler*

"Adolf Hitler?" said the youngish man. "It sounds very familiar, but I am almost positive it is not my name . . ."

"It must be you," said the bartender. "You even have a hitler mustache."

"What is a *hitler mustache*?" asked the man, feeling his face to find a strip of hair under his nose. "How do you know it is one?"

"I have never heard of Adolf Hitler the person, but I know all about hitler mustaches. My own son had one as a teenager."

"If I am Adolf Hitler then why would they name a mustache style after someone like me? Surely I am too young."

"You must be older than you look," said the bartender.

"But I do not *feel* old at all."

"You must be older than you feel," said the bartender.

The youngish man tried thinking again... *the mission, I am on a mission to track someone down, who?*

Then he checked his pockets... *there must be a picture or a notebook or papers somewhere that will assist me.* Dig-picking through the sandy bags. There was nothing.

"Is there a problem, Adolf?" asked the bartender.

"Do not call me Adolf," said the youngish man, rechecking the pockets, hesitation sweat.

Then he remembered...

"Briefcase," he said.

The bartender shrugged his eyebrows.

"I had a briefcase, where is it?"

"I did not see a briefcase."

"I had one..."

The youngish man scurried his eyes around the room, but the briefcase could not be found. His only link to the mission was lost... but there was something else lost that he was not remembering. With hard searching, he stumbled upon a memory. It flashed into his head like a piece of tape had been lying across his brain and was just then ripped away to expose the memory with exploding pain.

"My Partner?" he screamed, his voice echoed like flat soda. He shifted to the bartender. "Have you seen another man dressed like me? A slightly older man in a uniform such as this?"

The bartender shook his head. "I have never seen such a uniform in all my life."

"We were wandering in the desert ... Then he disappeared. He just vanished into nowhere."

"Did he just vanish into nowhere?" asked the bartender.

"Yes, he just vanished into nowhere."

The bartender looked away, his neck shifting like cloth. "Hmmm." He nodded and let out a frowning grunt. "A dakar spider must have gotten him."

"A *what*?"

"A dakar spider. It is a small insect with the ability to alter the mass of its prey. They can shrink anything as large as an elephant down to the size of a penny, making any creature a perfect victim. Your friend was probably standing near one when it shrank him down to helpless-size and captured him before he knew what was happening."

"You can not be saying that my partner was eaten by a little spider."

"It happens all the time."

The youngish man just shook his head, nerves twittering. The notion was scientifically implausible, but if such an absurd creature did exist it would explain his partner's disappearance.

"Well, have you seen another man?" he asked the bartender. "An imperfect man?"

"Imperfect? In what way?"

"I am not sure," he said. "I can not remember his face, but it is imperfect. He is a disease and I am here to cure society of him."

"No," said the bartender. "I have not seen any man/disease walking around. Maybe you should try Mrs. Neat.

She knows about everything that happens in this town. You can find her at the bakery in the morning."

"Where is the bakery?"

"You'll find it. Things are easy to find in this town. If you don't find it, then it will find you." Then he said, "Are you staying at the town's inn?"

"I do not know of any inn."

"It is the building next door. Mr. Wheel is probably still awake. He will give you a room for free if you have breakfast with him."

"I eat breakfast alone."

"Please eat breakfast with him. He is a very lonely man. He built that inn so he could be around people all the time, but not many people ever stay there. He is an awfully lonely man."

The youngish man nodded his head slowly, even though the thought of social dining turned his stomach. He thought, *the people in this town must be unaware that it is disgusting to eat outside the privacy of the home.*

"But what about my briefcase?" asked the youngish Hitler man.

"It will turn up eventually. Nothing ever stays lost around here."

Mr. Wheel

The night was plastic.
    The young Hitlerish man was staring up at the inn. It was a tall building. Not large, just lofty. Small in length and width but incredibly high, small room upon small room upon small room upon small room upon small room upon small room and so on into the plastic sky. The scarecrow building leaned over the drunken SS officer, like a monstrous mother facing her disobedient insect child. The sky behind was jet-ink and glassy clear. The clouds made creak-squeaking noises as they brushed against each other, similar to the rubbing together of birthday balloons.
    He staggered. His legs were not working right, as if one was longer than the other. Mash-minded, he plowed open the door of the inn with his face, his lips scratching the orange splintered wood.
    It was empty inside. There was nothing but cobwebs, boxes, closet emotions, and a lot of the color black. A cricky iron staircase was in the corner of the room. It spiraled up to the next floor, to an equal mass of black. There didn't seem to be anything in this building.
    The young Hitlerish man was worried. He looked

back to town. The houses surrounding him were dark. They all looked old and long abandoned. Shadows. Even the light in the tavern was dim and lifeless.

He held the door open as he entered, looking up the staircase to see if anyone was there. He put a rock in front of the door to keep the light inside, but the door rolled it aside with its ogre weight. The door shut behind him and the SS officer found himself trapped in the dark.

He took some steps with his hands leading, stretching towards the railing of the stairs. He heard noises behind the silence, squeaking. It must have been the plastic clouds outside. The air in the room prickled his arm hairs.

The railing bar landing in his palm was a relief, a safety bar. He began his ascent blindly, one step at a time, a pulsing sickness in his guts. Soon his eyes adjusted to the dimness and he could half-see the steps. As the first floor produced closet emotions, the second floor produced attic emotions. White blankets over furniture. The third floor produced basement emotions, with spider webs and a drip-dripping sound of water yet no sign of pipes. Then the fourth floor, a cold bathroom thick with mud and cracks, beady eyes from holes in the walls.

But the fifth floor came like a ghost to his ear. Advancing around the steps to it, the youngish man found a door blocking his way and there was a haunting strip of yellow light underneath. The light was proof that somebody actually lived here.

But it's so silent, he thought, *who would live in such a lonely deserted old building?*

"Mr. Wheel?" he called through the powdery door. No answer.

He knocked and opened the door to a dimly lit room filled with many shelves of dusty rusted antique dishes. A man was sitting by himself in the corner, carving small chess pieces from what looked to be the bones of a large animal. The youngish called again, "Mr. Wheel?"

The strange man shifted his ashen face to the Hitlerish officer. His skin was saggy and had cracks in it. The officer's brain nearly dropped out of his head once he noticed the white-white hair. He realized what this man was.

The youngish man said, "You are *old*?"

Mr. Wheel crook-grinned, then chuckled. "Well, that is the most impolite greeting I've ever heard." His voice as rusty and brittle as the antiques on the shelves.

The young officer sat down in a rickety chair in front of him to stare deeper.

"How can it be?" asked the officer. "It is illegal to live past the age of fifty."

The old man didn't seem to comprehend his drunken slurs.

"So you are staying the night?" asked Mr. Wheel. "It has been decades since I have seen a man of your age. Not since I was a child."

The young Hitlerish man was both overwhelmed and disgusted by his presence. He thought to himself: *How could the world allow him to be? Is he the imperfect man I am looking for? Could the destruction of a single old man be the entire goal of my mission?*

"Well," Mr. Wheel said. "It has been decades since I have *been* a man your age." His teeth were rotten, curly, when he laughed. It almost made the SS officer vomit to look upon him.

"Do you play chess?" asked the old man.

"Not since childhood," responded the officer.

"After breakfast, we should play chess."

The young Hitlerish officer didn't like the idea of playing chess with such a person. He was so *old*. And the thought of eating breakfast with him created banana-fibers to rise in his stomach and slide up his throat. Just the smell of the old man was making him sick.

"Are you okay, Adolf?" asked Mr. Wheel.

The young officer gag-coughed at him. "Adolf? You think I am Adolf Hitler, too?"

Perhaps Adolf Hitler really is my name, he wondered.

Mr. Wheel placed his lensless sunglasses onto his face to examine the young man's uniform. Actually, they were not lensless sunglasses. They were . . . *seeing* glasses.

"You are a freak!" cried young Adolf Hitler, snarling at his defective vision. "Defective vision is no longer allowed in our society. You are a history book that has forgotten where to end."

Mr. Wheel curled a grin. "You're an unusual character."

"Where am I?" asked young Adolf Hitler. "Is this Town? The bartender just ignored me when I asked him."

"Yes, the bartender does not have much of an attention span. Once I spoke to him for twenty minutes and he did not even realize I was there. Oh, I can't wait to play chess in the morning. It is such a good and challenging game."

Adolf's head was weak. It swayed to the side and then around. He needed to sleep. He needed to put himself together.

"I am looking for a man," blurted the youngish officer. "He is an *imperfect* man."

"Imperfect? In what way?"

"I am not sure," Adolf said. "I can not remember his face, but it is imperfect. He is a disease and I am here to cure society of him."

"I don't think I've seen an imperfect man anywhere . . ."

"Well, *you* are imperfect. You are *old*."

"Am I the man you are looking for?"

"I do not believe you are a threat to the Nation, so I conclude that you are not him. The man I seek is riddled with ill genes that can pollute the human race if he is to reproduce."

"He sounds awful," said Mr. Wheel. "I would sure like to help you, but I haven't a clue where to look. I haven't seen such a monster anywhere in town."

"He must be stopped." Young Adolf Hitler squeezed a fist.

A shriek-blasting scream and a thousand footsteps scampered across the ceiling.

Nerves scurried up young Adolf's spine. "What is that?"

The old man hushed him, held his shoulder for calming.

The strange noise halted in the corner of the ceiling and softened, turned into whimpers, twisted rat cries.

Mr. Wheel whispered, "She is always restless at

this time."

"Who?"

"Elsie, my daughter. She has these mood swings."

"Mood swings?"

"She has not taken to the idea of being dead yet."

"She is dead?"

The old man pulled his neck down as the girl's voice shrieked through the air at the officer, as if it was attacking him.

"Don't mention her death," said Mr. Wheel. "It upsets her."

"How can she make those noises when she is dead?"

"That is the problem, she doesn't realize she is dead."

"What is wrong with this place?" said the officer. "There is no order here. This town is so unorganized that it allows its dead to throw temper tantrums?"

"It is not so bad," whispered Mr. Wheel.

He silenced young Adolf Hitler before he could continue to complain.

Quiet, quiet.

After some time, Elsie's cries dissolved into the woodwork as the SS officer's eyes began fading . . .

Mr. Wheel pushed him awake, "You are falling asleep there, Adolf. Maybe you should go up to bed."

Adolf's voice was as hazy as his eyes. "I want to, but . . ."

"Do not worry about Elsie. She does not hurt a fly. I will take you."

Mr. Wheel pulled him from the chair with surprising strength and took him up the spiral staircase.

"But you are going to have to look out for dakar spiders," said Mr. Wheel. "The inn is infested."

"Dakar spiders?" Adolf tried to free himself from his arm.

"You are safer from them here than anywhere else."

They went up to the tenth floor, the top floor, and the old man put young Adolf on a large fuzzy bed. The aluminum door rumbled like thunder when he closed it behind him.

The Hitlerish man entered the musty sheets. They had not been washed in years. Dust was rising from the bed, dancing up in the faint window light.

There were webs all around the bed, but the youngish man took them for cobwebs. He felt it was best not to think about the dakar spider, though he was sure that such a thing was too absurd to really exist.

It must be a local superstition, he thought. *What a sad place to still have superstitions . . .*

Absorbed in grogginess, young Hitler did not care that the sheets were meaty-rancid and stale or that the room was murky and dungeon-like. All he wanted was sleep.

Just as his eyes rolled into closure, he noticed that someone was sleeping beside him.

Mr. Sausage

Sleeping next to young Adolf Hitler was a whale of a man, sprawled across the pirate ship blankets with a guzzling snore.

A *fat* man.

Hitler could smell his sweaty rolls, the stench seeping through the fabrics, polluting his air. It was disgusting. Hitler sat up. Stared crinkle-faced at the man.

The officer hit him, pounded flubbering waves throughout him like a waterbed. His breathing paused. Then continued. Hitler's teeth began to grind.

"Get out of my bed!" he hiss-whispered at the large mound/man. He hit him again, shoved him with his heels under the rot-covers.

The large man did not move. Adolf kicked again, trying to push him off the mattress.

"Get off, you fat sweaty animal!"

Still, he would not budge nor waken.

"He will not get up," said a voice from within the room.

The officer jerked his head, scanning the shadowy corners of the room. A young woman in night clothes seeped out of the woodwork. She floated through the cobwebs and dirt piles towards him.

"He never gets up," she said.

"Who are you?" Adolf asked.

"I am Mr. Wheel's daughter," she responded.

"Elsie?"

"Yes," she answered. "Who are you?"

"I do not know," said the officer. "I have lost all of my memory."

"Have you?" Elsie asked, leaning against the mattress, glaring close to his chest. "You are *Adolf Hitler*."

"I am *not* Adolf Hitler," responded the young Hitlerish man.

"But you have *Adolf Hitler* written on your uniform..."

"Yes, but I also have *God* written on my uniform, and I am certainly not God."

"But maybe you *are* God."

"I highly doubt that God would lose his memory as I have."

"So you have no idea who you are?"

"Not a clue."

"Maybe you are *Adolf Hitler*..."

"Perhaps, but I do not have time to prove my identity right now. I must move this large man so that I can sleep, and I must sleep so that I can find my briefcase in the morning, and I must find my briefcase so that I can get a photograph, and I must get the photograph so that I will know who the man is that I am hunting."

"Who is this man you are hunting?" asked the ghost girl.

"He is an *imperfect* man."

"Imperfect? In what way?"

"I am not sure," said the officer. "I can not remember his face, but it is imperfect. He is a disease and I am here to . . ."

"Is *he* your imperfect man?" Elsie asked, pointing at the whale/man nearby.

"Well," he began, "he is definitely imperfect, but his genes are not wrong. Being overweight might be illegal, but it is not a threat to the purity of the human race."

She stared down with her glossy eyes, not knowing what else to say.

Young Hitler was very tired and perplexed. His mind was sidetracked and he just then realized that he was conversing with a dead girl. She began rude-gawking at him, examining his little mustache, her little lips grinning. The officer didn't know what to say. Mr. Wheel had told him that she did not like to realize that she had died, so the youngish man did not bring it up to her.

"I am not a ghost," Elsie said.

Adolf paused, hesitated to speak.

"My father says that I am dead, but I am not," she said. "Feel."

The ghost girl took his hand and pressed it to her chest, and asked, "Do I feel like a dead woman to you?"

She was cold, icy-skinned with tight-flesh rather than flexible. Her skin was paper-white, bloodless.

"No," he answered, his hand shivering against her cruel skin. "You are very much alive."

She smiled, happy with his decision, bouncing slightly in excitement, but she did not release his hand from her skin.

"The whole town says that I am dead, but we both know I am not. They are all very mistaken. Just because I can walk through walls does not mean that I am dead."

"But people are going to think you are a ghost if you walk through walls in front of them," said the officer, trying to pull his hand from her grip.

"Tell me about it . . . The cockroach people scream bloody murder every time I enter their walls."

"The cockroach people?" His hand went numb from her cold skin.

"They are the little ones who live between the walls. They are half bug and half human."

"*These* walls," he pointed with his free hand, nervous.

"Yes, *all* walls. They are human infestations."

"How disgusting . . ." he commented.

Elsie paused, stared away from him for a sigh. She released his cold-burned hand to squeeze closer to him, press some of her parts against his parts. Lightning shivered up his spine. Then he noticed that she was crawling into bed with him.

"What are we going to do about *him*?" Elsie asked about the morbidly obese man.

Adolf looked around. "I do not know, but I need to sleep."

"Me too," she said. "And I do not think that all three of us will fit comfortably in this bed."

"All three of us?" Adolf asked, his voice growing in strength.

"Well, this is *my* bed," said Elsie. "Many years ago

this whale-man fell asleep in my bed and would not wake or leave, so I have been stuck sleeping next to him every night for as long as I can remember."

"YEARS AGO? He has not starved to death?"

Elsie shrugged. "He must be living off of his body weight, hibernating."

"I do not know how we can all sleep in one bed. Surely, there are other beds in this inn."

"Move over," Elsie said. "Let me lie down."

She lifted the sour-blankets and pushed her way inside. Her icy body pressed completely against his with ticklings, and shoved him into the fat of the whale/man. After touching his skin, young Adolf Hitler realized that the morbidly obese man was not clothed. Trapped between icy stiff skin and sweaty, fat, naked flesh, the officer didn't know whether he should vomit or scream.

"I will help you find your briefcase in the morning," Elsie said. "We will go to the Bakery. Mrs. Neat is sure to know where it is. She knows everything."

Her cold legs rubbed against his, maybe for warmth, maybe for quick physical sensation. She soon fell asleep next to him. His body was comfortable to her, but her body was like razorblades to him.

It took three hours for Hitler's eyes to get groggy again. They slid halfway shut, but then opened. Even though he was more tired than he had ever been, he could not fall asleep. He lay pondering, trying to remember his real name and the face of the imperfect man. Nothing came to mind.

Three more hours went by. Three hours of numb skin on his left side and sticky skin on his right. He could not sleep. Three more hours. He was expecting the sun to come up, but the sky was still night outside. *Was time moving slower than usual?* he thought. *Did I forget how many hours are in one night?* Three more hours. It was getting ridiculous. He almost laughed at his situation. Trapped between a hibernating obese man and a living dead girl, not being able to sleep, and not being able to wake up because the day was not arriving.

Three more hours.

He gave up, got out of bed, out of the covers and stepped over the fat man, careful not to touch him. The freedom was satisfying, his left arm warming and his right drying off. But then he didn't know what to do, standing there without a purpose. He looked out of the window to find some sign of the sun, but there was nothing. The moon was dead-center in the sky, not going down, not making room for morning. The town was still shadowed. He could see a few profiled buildings, but nothing within the murk. No lights were on. He felt alone.

He must have stood there for another three hours. Confused, hesitating to do anything. He curled up into a ball on the ground, in the dust and cobwebs. Water dropped from his eyes but he could not tell if he was crying or perspiring.

After a few minutes, his eyes rolled shut, his thoughts rolled back into his brain. He didn't remember being asleep, but he must have been; for at least a few minutes or it could have been hours. His eyes jerked open, bringing him out of whatever dream he was having, just before something metal clubbed him in the back of the head.

Mr. Nothing

Besides the sleeping ghost girl and sweaty fat man, young Adolf Hitler was alone in the room. Swelling bloody bruises grew beneath his head hairs. He could not comprehend who had hit him.

There was nothing. He scanned the room to find nothing in the cracks between the floorboards, nothing behind or beneath the squeaky mattress box, nothing against the wall, nothing floating in the air with the rising dust. There was so much of nothing in the room that it felt like *nothing* was a living individual.

The blood was hot and tickled his skin. Adolf watched the soft snoring of the whale/man, wondering if he had been the one to club him in the back of the head with a blunt metal object. Perhaps the morbidly obese man was just pretending to be asleep.

Hitler slimed his muscles as he stepped to the door and opened it to more darkness and more nothing. The attacker was not here, either. Creeping the stairwell, he took steps down to a lower floor and opened its door. Another bedroom. Almost identical to the one above but the bed was made of charcoal and dust. It must have been set on fire some time ago. He looked for a bathroom. There wasn't one here.

A faint blue light emanated from underneath the door of the next room down. Hitler's thoughts went dizzy as he grabbed the knob. But it didn't turn.

Locked?

He turned the other way. It shifted an inch then stopped. It wasn't locked, just jammed. He placed his shoulder along the frame and turned the knob until sharp veiny muscles popped out of his arm, then pushed his weight against the door. A cracking noise and then it broke open.

Needle-shriek noises assaulted him as he entered. Hundreds of insect-things scurried across the floor into the walls. The shiny moon reflected blue paint off the wall and scattered it across the carpeting and bed.

There was a skeleton sleeping on the bed. The officer peered into its ribcage to see dozens of faces staring back at him. Insect people, hiding, shivering at him like he was about to squish them.

The disgusting creatures deserve to be squished, thought Hitler. *They are atrocious and should be exterminated like all other vermin.*

He rubbed his head wound and stepped back, turned around to find a sink on the wall. It wasn't a bathroom, but the bedroom had a sink and a mirror. He unzipped the fly on his uniform and urinated into the sink. The odor from the dusty bones and tiny people feces steamed up his nostrils and made him want to exit the room immediately, but he had to wash his head wound and clean dirt from his face and hands.

"Why is this place such an abomination?" he asked the mirror.

His once perfect blond hair was ruined with blood. His uniform was filth-ridden and suffering.

The mirror did not respond.

"I came here to find a single threat to the human race but I have found an entire town of them. How can this place exist?"

The mirror did not respond.

A miniature woman crawled out from behind the faucet knob and stood on the sink, facing Adolf. She hugged her dress to her bosom — a strip of blanket fabric with a hole in the center for her head to go through, covering her front and back but exposing the sides of her breasts.

The little woman began to move on the porcelain, wiggling and jagged-turning.

"What is that you are doing?" young Hitler asked the little woman. "Are you dancing?"

She spun around and the fabric lifted to show me her filthy sex parts.

"That is not dancing," he told her. "Your movements are too chaotic. They have no rhythm. Dancing must be organized and calculated to be beautiful. Your motions are disgusting."

He flicked her across the room with his middle finger and she made a squee noise as she soared through the air.

"Horrible creature," he said.

The hundreds of insect people began to scream at young Hitler from around the bed, roaring angry revenge. Perhaps the miniature woman didn't survive the fall.

"You are only bugs," he told them, and went back to the mirror.

Adolf's reflection made him wince. His appearance was less than acceptable. Ugliness and chaos surrounded him and it was causing him to change into something disgusting. He had no memory. That made him flawed, wrong. He deserved execution. There had to be a way to reunite himself with the knowledge of himself and the mission.

"I am not this Adolf Hitler person," he said. "Or am I?"

He brought his palm to the mirror to rub the reflection, but it did not hit the cold surface. Instead, his hand fell through. It was not a normal mirror. It was another abomination.

"It must be broken or flawed."

He pierced his face through the mirror to see a room identical to the one he was standing in.

"What is this?" he asked the room. "The mirror's reflection is tangible. Like it is three-dimensional instead of two. How can this be?"

He crawled through and became one with his own reflection in the mirror. His features reversed themselves. He was now left-handed. His heart was on the other side of his chest. His swastika band switched arms.

The insect people were not in the bed on this side. Their reflections were hiding. Adolf left the room, still in the reflection, and went upstairs to the bedroom. He hoped the reflections of the whale man and the ghost girl were missing so that he could get some sleep.

Upon entry, he noticed that all the smells were absent, the dust covering the floor seemed painted on. There were two figures on the bed, but there were no snores coming from them. One did not seem as sweaty and one did not seem as cold.

Hitler's breath went chirpy out of his lungs as he noticed the two bedmates were not actually human. He touched one of them. Light crispy skin. They were made out of balls of newspaper, crumpled up, compacted to form their figures.

"Fake," he said. "Like dolls or—"

Some movement broke his speech. Something was coming out of the darkness, shambling, crackling. It leapt from the shadows at Adolf with swirling claws. There were several of them lunging at him from all angles.

Hitler jerk-fell and rolled away. He found himself outside the room, tumbling downstairs with the dark things coming after him.

His vision caught a slight glimpse of one: teethy, spiky black children without legs or arms. Just claws, mouth, and fire-eyes. Snarling like distant thunder.

He burst into the room he started from and crawled out of the mirror, ripping the knee of his uniform against the metal sink. He looked back. They didn't follow him. All he saw was his own face looking back at him.

Mr. Eyebrows

"I heard your scream," Elsie said, entering the room as young Hitler watched his reflection carefully.

Adolf didn't remember screaming.

"You shouldn't be in my mother's room," she said.

"There are creatures in there that attacked me," he yelled at her, pointing at the mirror.

"Of course you are going to get attacked if you wander too far into the walk-in mirror," Elsie said. "The sadness demons hate it when you invade their territory."

"Sadness demons? I have never heard of such things. I have also never heard of walk-in mirrors. They are abominable."

"Sadness demons live inside of mirrors in the places you can't see. Like behind furniture or around corners."

"But I did not see them behind furniture. I went into the reflection, then out the door, then up the stairs back to the room where they were hiding in shadows."

"Yes, the upstairs room is beyond the reflection, so the sadness demons can live there. They have their own world, on the other side of mirrors. They do not appreciate invaders."

"That is an abomination. Mirrors are meant to reflect the beauty of Man, not house the putridness of demons."

"It is true. Not many people know about them because they can't go into their mirrors. But these mirrors are three-dimensional, so you can. They were invented by the Golden Eel."

"Who is the Golden Eel?" asked the officer.

"He is the mayor of this town and everybody loves him."

"What kind of man has a name like the Golden Eel?"

"It is not a man. It is an eel made out of gold."

"Are you saying an eel runs this town? No wonder it is an abomination! An eel can not even do menial labor . . ."

A memory flashed into his head: one of working as a child.

He remembered working in factories and as a food server as a young boy. All children were forced to do the hard, low-paying work. A century ago, the lower classes would work menial jobs and children played after school. Then the Fuhrer eliminated all the impure people, which happened to include the entire lower class, so there were no people left to work the undesirable jobs but children.

All boys and girls between the ages of five and seventeen were forced to work menial labor for eight hours a day, go to school for eight more, and try to combine homework, chores, eating, and sleeping during the last eight. It proved to build character in young people. It built strength and responsibility, prepared them for the world beyond childhood. The world of efficiency and perfection.

That was why this place made Hitler sick. He had never experienced inefficiency before. He was not ready for it. It is utterly uncomfortable to him.

"I have to get out of here," he told the ghost girl.

"Yes, please get out. You are disturbing Mother." The girl motioned to the corpse on the bed as she pulled Adolf into the hall, saying, "We must go to sleep."

"I tried, but I could not."

"I can never sleep either, but I like to lie down and close my eyes for long periods of time. Come sleep with me?"

"I do not have time for sleep anymore. It should be morning any second anyway."

Elsie replied, "Morning is probably still a very long time away."

"What do you mean? This night has gone on for maybe a dozen hours. It *must* be morning soon."

"But the sun is erratic and unpredictable. It comes up whenever it does. It can rise a minute from now or it might come up a year from now. There's no schedule."

"Are you saying this town doesn't even have order in its day and night?"

"The sun moves at random. Actually, it's been probably a few years since it last set."

"What? You mean I might be stuck in this night for years? For ever?"

"Possibly, or maybe just for a few more seconds, you never know. There's no rules to it."

"This place is an abomination! It does not even have a sun in the sky when it is supposed to be there. Man relies on the sun's regularity. You can not rely on randomness."

Then the ghost girl touched her cold hand to his forehead, breaking him from the subject. Adolf jerked away.

"Why are you touching me?"

"You're bleeding."

"Yes, I was clubbed over the head with a blunt metal object earlier and I am not sure who hit me."

"It must have been Mr. Eyebrows."

"Mr. Eyebrows?"

"He is a ghost who is in love with me. He doesn't care that I'm not a ghost like him."

"Why did he hit me?"

"He is always jealous of my boyfriends."

"Oh," Hitler said, nodding.

He didn't yet realize that she just called him her boyfriend.

Mrs. Ghost

"Can we sleep together now?" said the ghost girl.

"Is Mr. Eyebrows going to club me again?"

She kicked her foot through the floor and said, "He won't bother you as long as you're with me."

"I will not sleep with you. I must find another bed."

"They are all occupied."

"By whom?"

"Other guests."

"Other guests? Are they all ghosts? I only see ghosts."

"Are you calling me a ghost?"

"I am calling nobody a ghost."

"Are you calling me a ghost?"

"I just meant that this hotel is like a graveyard. It is old and like death."

"Oh, well that is because it is night. During the day it is much more lively. The night is all shadows and old men."

"I do feel like I am in a world of old men. Where I am from, we do not have old men. We outlawed them because they do not function effectively anymore at that age and also because they are uncomfortable to be around."

"Do you think I'm pretty?" asked the ghost girl.

Eyebrowing her. "You are a child."

"I'm seventeen," she roared. "I'm old enough to have children."

"You are just a child. You should be working in a shoe factory."

"So you don't want to go back to bed with me?" Her eyes grew moist and wide.

"I'd rather sleep with the mirror demons."

Then she exploded. Adolf knew his statement would make her sad or maybe angry, but the girl went berserk.

Her body became icy globs of energy, her facial features melted outward, her mouth opened up around her head. Then she stormed into Hitler, her entire body crawling in through his belly button, and melting out through his back. She shrieked down the stairs and through the walls, spreading her mass until it dissipated into the air and she became a part of the building.

Then she was just the cracklings in the wooden floors, tappings in the glass of the windows.

Young Hitler's skin was wrinkled from her icy entry. Tensed muscles, teeth locked. He couldn't help but remain standing there in a heap of shivers, frozen.

His brain was full of wasps.

Mr. Wheel

He should've just gone to sleep with the whale/man, but decided against it. His head was still scrambled, dizzy from all of the chaos he'd been going through. The last thing he wanted to do was get back into that horrible disease-infested bed. So he went searching for an empty bedroom.

Hesitating at every doorknob, looking for one that would open. No luck. He continued down the stairs trying every room. All of the doors were locked. He imagined other guests asleep in these haunted rooms, like the whale/man.

But didn't the bartender say that nobody ever stays at the inn? Maybe these rooms are filled with more corpses. Corpses and ghosts and obese men . . .

Adolf found himself in the room of Mr. Wheel again. The elderly person was still awake, sitting in a smoky orange-fur chair with his shirt off. The officer shuddered at the old man's nude torso. The wrinkled old flesh made him cringe, but there was something even worse about Mr. Wheel's nudity that nearly made Hitler cry out in horror.

There was a wooden door on the old man's chest

where his nipples should have been, and the door was opened to reveal his insides. His insides were gruesome and unreal. There weren't any internal organs. There were only globs of gooey meat between rusty metal gears. His innards looked like the insides of clocks. The elderly man was fixing his decrepit heart with a screwdriver and pliers, twisting bolts, popping gadgets into place.

"So this is what it is to be an old man," Adolf cried at him, spitting at a muddy landscape painting on the wall. "You are forced to repair yourself like an automobile engine."

Mr. Wheel blushed and slammed the door to his chest, like his insides were private.

"I didn't hear you come in." His voice weasely and dusty.

"You are a disgusting old man."

Mr. Wheel smiled in response. "Yes, I suppose I can be on the unsettling side. It is very easy to become disgusting after age has its way with you."

Crickets pig-squealed in the corners as Adolf stepped closer to him.

"Why are you not insulted? Are you so weak that you accept disdain like a gift?"

"No, no," said the old man. "I'm just being understanding. Open-minded."

"Open-minded?" Adolf snorted. Then he shook his head and asked, "Do you have another room? Mine is unacceptable."

The old man tapped his wrist. "No, I'm sorry but you have the only unoccupied room."

"Are you mocking me? That room is occupied by

the ghost of your dead daughter and the fattest man in the universe."

"Oh," Mr. Wheel smacked his shiny forehead. "I completely forgot they sleep there. I'm terribly sorry. Perhaps you would like to sit down and play chess with me while waiting for the bed to become vacant?"

"I must sleep, Mr. Wheel. I am on a very important mission and do not have time for chess. I am looking for the imperfect man."

"Imperfect?" asked Mr. Wheel. "In what way?"

"I am not sure," said the officer. "I can not remember his face, but it is imperfect. He is a disease and I am here to cure society of him."

"Yes, I remember now. Well, sit down and we will play chess."

"But I must sleep. You will rid the bed of the obese man at once."

"Oh, he should be up one of these days soon. He is the town doctor."

"The doctor?"

How can such an unhealthy man be a doctor?

"Yes, he told me to wake him if there is a medical emergency."

"Has there been?"

"No, not at all. Everyone is asleep. There aren't usually medical emergencies when everyone is asleep. In the morning he will wake."

"But when will morning come?"

"Someday soon, I believe. It hasn't been morning for years, but it can come at any second. In the meantime we will play chess. Come here."

Adolf did as Mr. Wheel asked, but only because his legs were tired of holding him up. He sat down in a chair made out of old encyclopedias. Unfortunately for young Adolf, Mr. Wheel thought the act of his sitting down was an agreement to play chess with him.

The old man took a chess board out of a fur case and set it on a red stool between them. Then he took out the playing pieces which were not so much chess pieces as they were morbid works of art. Squishy noises when he placed them on the chess board.

"What is this?" Adolf asked.

"A game of strategy!" cried Mr. Wheel.

The pieces were individual bundles of rubbery meat and tendons. All the pawns were topped with wet goat eyeballs. The king was a large blob of fatty steak meat and the queen was a cat paw covered in rose thorns. The bishop looked like a severed penis, erect and bleeding, while the knight looked like a vagina molded into the shape of a horse. But the rook was the oddest piece. It looked like four fingers tied together with teeth growing from the finger tips. And near the base of the piece there seemed to be a sweaty mouth, breathing and licking at itself.

"Ready?" asked Mr. Wheel. "You start."

Hitler didn't start.

The pieces were sizzling, pulsing and making pop-pop noises. Some were even foaming onto the chess board. The officer's face turned white once the greasy smell slithered up his nostrils.

"Well?" asked the impatient Mr. Wheel, clenching fists in anticipation.

Hitler squished his fingers into a middle pawn,

Adolf in Wonderland

cum-slippery in his hands. He moved two spaces up and let it slide out of his fingers into place. The piece sweated a puddle inside its new square.

Even chess, the most symmetrical and perfect game ever invented, is ruined in this dreadful town.

Mr. Wheel moved his pawn to meet Hitler's. His fingers were coated in foam that he licked off with his rough white tongue.

"Why am I being tortured like this?" young Hitler asked Mr. Wheel, pausing the game with a hard face.

Mr. Wheel was strategizing and paid no mind.

Adolf said, "I do not deserve to be in such calamity. I am in hell here."

"It's your move," said Mr. Wheel.

"I am going back upstairs," the officer told him.

"But we have yet to finish," Mr. Wheel cried. "Please, Adolf..."

"Adolf is not my name."

"Then what is your name?"

"I do not know, but it is probably not Adolf Hitler."

"But Adolf Hitler is written on your shirt?"

"Yes, but God is also written on my shirt, and I am certainly not God."

"But maybe you *are* god?"

"I doubt that God would lose His memory as I have."

"Then perhaps you are food for the dakar spider?"

"What does that mean?"

"Oh yes, dakar spiders have the ability to steal memories of potential prey. They do this to disorient you, make you easier to hunt and kill."

"What place is this that has its insects at the top of

the food chain? They are but tiny pests which man has the right to step on."

Mr. Wheel snickered. "I wouldn't try to step on a dakar spider if I were you."

"This is pure insanity! I can not believe you are trying to convince me that there is a tiny spider out there that is planning to eat me."

"Once it is hungry enough, yes."

"You, sir, are an abomination!"

"Can we get on with this game?" asked Mr. Wheel. "Or are you afraid of being beaten by an old man?"

"I am going upstairs to sleep."

"But what about the doctor?"

"I will throw him from the bed if I have to."

At the door, Mr. Wheel got in a couple lines: "Watch out for the dakar spider. They love to attack humans in their sleep."

And in the hallway, young Hitler cried, "Ridiculous! Pure lunacy!"

Mrs. Perfect

Young Adolf Hitler heard churking clockwork sounds as he hiked up the stairs, probably Mr. Wheel's hands going back into his chest to repair his faulty insides.

"I am in my coffin," he said to the dust rising on the narrow stairs.

Then he paused. He looked down at a piece of mirror by his feet and saw himself looking up at him.

"Are you giving up?" he asked himself.

He grabbed his uniform by the collar, "Is that what you are doing? Giving up? Is a man of perfection to be overtaken and defeated by the chaotic?"

Adolf's arm raised upward, sieg heiling the top of the staircase as if he was saluting God — the most perfect being in all the universe.

This was what he was thinking:

I am flawless.

I will not allow the weak to overcome me.

I will find the impure man and the nation will be clean of imperfections forever!

Then he heard crying from the upstairs room. A

woman's sniffles and wails.

He could smell rain.

Ascending to the room, his leg bones felt like they were made out of wood from the lack of sleep. There was a strange woman on the bed. Not Elsie, but someone else. Elsie was not there, nor the whale/man.

Was this even the same room I was in before?

The woman on the bed had her face buried into her knees, naked under the blankets. She had long blond hair in locks like golden waterfalls rivering from her scalp. The blond hair was a comforting sight to Young Adolf.

His voice went soft, "Why are you crying?"

She raised her face. Ocean blue eyes, moonlight skin.

The face of an angel . . .
She is like me. She is perfection.
Then his mind clicked.

There was something familiar about her. She was someone he knew, someone from his past. But his memories were covered in fuzz.

"I'm crying because I missed you," said the woman with a wet tongue.

Adolf's mind was racing: *who is she? is she my girlfriend? ex-girlfriend? wife? how could she know me? what is she doing here in this town?*

"Come to me," the woman said.

Her arms opened, exposing her perfect breasts. Young Adolf went to her.

"I have no memory," he told her.

"Don't speak," she hushed him, "you're always talking . . ."

She pressed him against her warm skin, perfect body against his filthy uniform. Her hands crawled his back, walking the ribs with her fingers, and then she wrapped them up in a big furry blanket that was full of dust and fat man smell and dead bugs but Hitler didn't seem to care.

He was in a dream. He had found home, even though he didn't recognize it.

Mr. D

Her arms around him and he was shivering in her warmth. Her legs of hot steel gripped him into her.

His eyebrows snuggled against her face.

He went to wrap her body closer, but as soon as she touched his chest her body became thin like it was liquifying. Her face shriveled and she slipped through his arms, sucked down into the dirty mattress. Shrinking.

A scream like lava from Hitler's throat as he realized what had happened. He searched the bed for her . . .

She must be small like a bug now, lost in an ocean of blankets.

And as he ripped through the bedding, he felt the blankets rise up over his head, growing into a mass of bearskins. Then he found himself suffocating, buried beneath a million pounds of cloth.

The blanket world was dim and filthy. And Hitler wasn't alone . . .

Something was piling towards him, crashing through the sheets. His brain collapsed as it crawled into view: a forest of spiky blackness.

It was an elephant-sized spider with large lobster

claws and snail-eyes, with large rubber hoses running from its head to its abdomen.

When Hitler ran, he had to push the covers up over his head to get through. Push-rolling his way under the soggy bedding as the spider came at him with fizzle sounds, choking wheezes.

His movement was very slow but the spider could not catch him. The sheets moving up and down created vibrations all around the spider. It got confused and couldn't tell exactly where the shrunken man was in the bed.

Then the floor vanished underneath Hitler's feet and he found himself sliding down the inside of the blanket, almost freefalling. He hit what felt like a wooden bird's nest, knocking the wind out of him and blood trickled from his lower lip. It was not wood but a blanket, a fluffy pile of blanket.

When he got to his feet Adolf was under the bed, a hundred stories beneath. Black wine smells as he gazed into the enormous under-bed, just waiting for the dakar spider to come hopping down after him.

It didn't come.

His eyes were red and tearing. His whole body trembled with tiny involuntary whines.

Adolf staggered away from the blanket, through the dark cavernous under-bed. His thoughts were a confusing blur. He didn't know what to make of what had just happened to him. For some reason, his thoughts were visions of hollowed out angels.

A while later, once he composed himself a bit, Adolf wandered out from under the bed and into the open.

The room was a new universe to him. A whole world of its own, full of mountainous brown-glowing furniture and storybook textures.

There were no longer closet emotions here. It was now ocean-like. So vast it was hard for him to breathe. Not as beautiful as the ocean, but just as powerful. An enormous swamp-world of dust and splinters.

In the distance the dakar spider was beginning to descend from a bedpost on a long silvery strand of web.

"I am not an insect," young Adolf told the dakar spider, "I am a pure and flawless man, just one hundredth the size."

He strolled away with a high chin and snapped his finger at a fluffy winter sock. "What is my name?" he asked the sock. "I must have my memory back or my mission will be a failure."

Warmth wrapped around him from behind. He could tell it was his lover, the perfect woman from his forgotten past.

He turned to her and asked, "Who am I?"

She smiled and caressed his cheek.

"Adolf Hitler," she responded.

PART TWO
Down the Rabbit Hole

PART TWO
Design as a Political Force

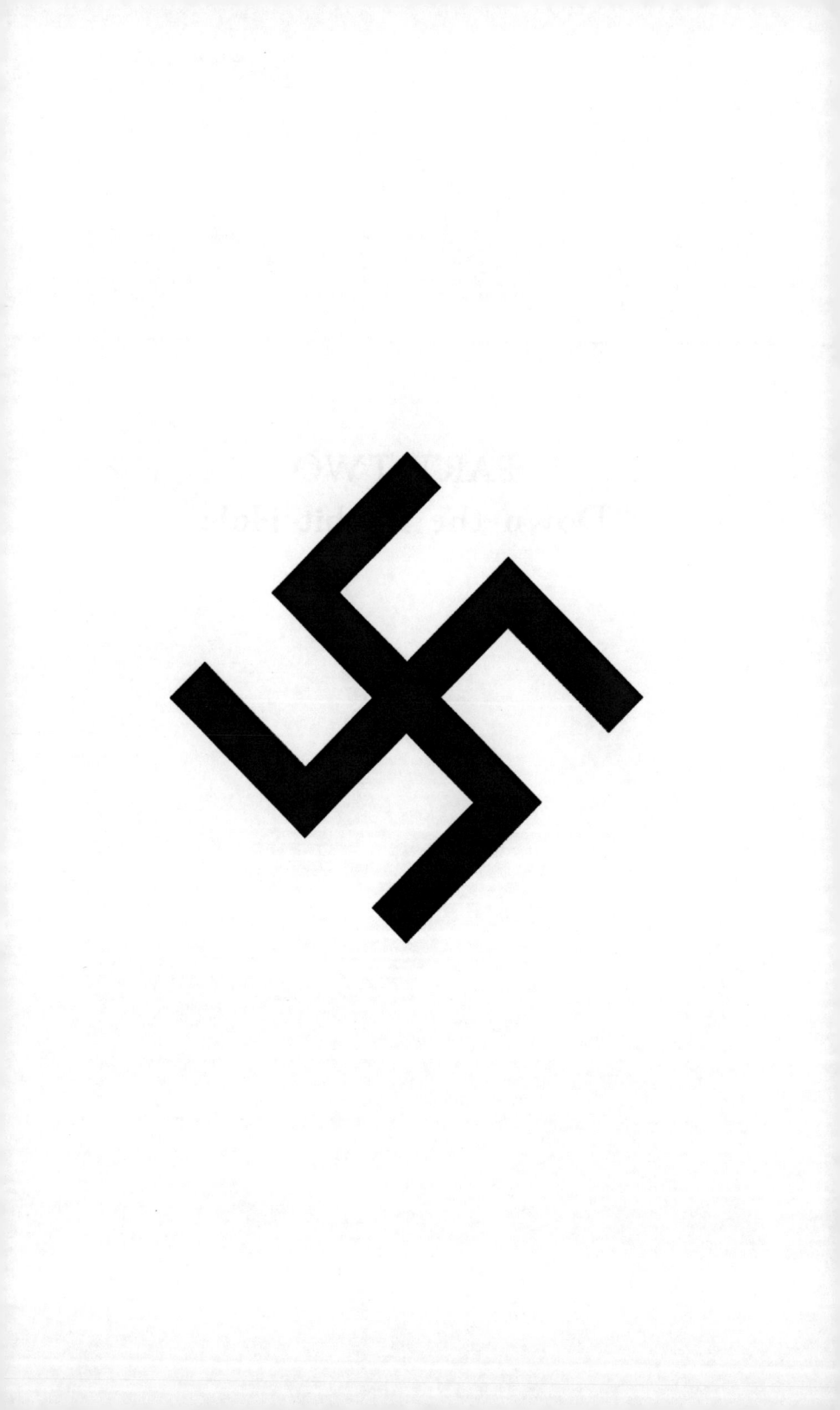

Mr. Small

The sky was wrinkled and brown. A moonbeam smiled through the window, giving their skin an appearance of glowing porcelain.

The shrunken couple crept slowly through the room, looking high into the sky. Way up there, somewhere, was a ceiling but all they could see was brown jagged swirls. There was movement in the air. Things were oozing in and out of the dark. Adolf looked carefully. Then he saw long squid-spikes and speckled flying snakes curling through the air, dancing in the moonlight.

Adolf wondered if these were things that could only be seen from the perspective of miniature creatures. Perhaps they are invisible to the regular-sized human eye. Then he wondered if perhaps his brain had become damaged from being compressed. Perhaps these were just illusions.

No, that is impossible. My brain is incapable of producing hallucinations. My theory of smallness being able to detect that which is invisible to the naked eye is quite reasonable. It is like looking under a microscope, but what I am witnessing here is not bacteria or germs. It is something invisible even to the microscope's eye. Not because of smallness, but for some other reason. Perhaps being this small allows me to see between dimensions, or perhaps these are just more abominable flaws created by this unstable town.

Their footsteps sounded unusual as they walked. They did not make the creaking wood sounds as before. Their steps were loud taps like dropping needles on tin.

"Where do we go?" the woman asked.

"I don't know," Hitler said. "We can't get down the stairs in our current condition."

"The dakar spider is still after us . . ."

"The dakar spider is an abomination and I refuse to acknowledge such a creature," he said.

Adolf folded his arms at her.

They cautious-stepped into the darkness of the room. The dark corners of this world/room were coated thick with dust and webs. There seemed to be even more of them now that he was small. The webs were silvery mountains, freckled with blood-red pods and green gluey tentacles that drooped into the path in front of them.

"There's a hole," the woman said, pointing to a blob of black between the hills of web.

"I do not trust webs," Adolf told her.

"We don't have a choice," she said.

She walked forward, dipping under some green vines and twisty tentacles. Hitler followed. They tap-tapped their way through the webworld, walking underneath purple hands that dangled from threads above. There were bundles of white in the web, some of them half-opened to reveal tiny human skeletons, hanging silent in the stiff air.

Adolf glanced at another bundle of web. A large

one. The contents were alive within, breathing, snoring. He stopped. Stared closer. He saw a part of him hanging out, gurgling his breath. It was the whale/man who had occupied the bed earlier. The dakar spider must have shrunk him in his sleep and brought him up into these spider hills, as preserved food for later. The morbidly obese man snuggled comfortably in the web. He seemed undisturbed despite all that had happened to him.

Now I know where he disappeared to when I left the room, Adolf thought.

Though Elsie was also gone.

Did the dakar spider get her too. Can ghosts be eaten by spiders? It seems impossible, but it is also impossible for there to be such a thing as ghosts or spiders that shrink people.

"We should hurry," the woman said, pulling the officer from his frozen stare.

They hurried until arriving at a hole in the wall. It was a soggy hole, created from water eating through the wood. A rancid sauce sweated across the floor at their feet. The smell offended Hitler's senses.

"What if there is a spider in there?" he asked her.

He already knew the answer to that question and her frowning facial expression of a response only strained his nerves further.

"Let's go," she pulled him forward, leading the way, holding his hand tight so that they did not separate.

Soon they were within pure blackness. All of their senses were suffocated by hot moisture and rotten smells. After several minutes of wandering blindly, slipping in mold and brushing against cobwebs, they saw a light up ahead. They even heard sounds that could have been human voices. They went towards the light until they arrived in a small room at the end of the tunnel.

Mr. Handlebar Mustache

The room was small, small enough to touch the ceiling even in their micro-state. The walls crackled and bubbled with a foamy gray mold. On one side of the room, there was a door. A miniature plastic door designed for tiny dolls. In the center of the room, there was a pile of acid-goo, sizzling and breathing and glowing green like a firefly. It produced warmth and emitted an intense yeasty fish odor that attacked Hitler's nostrils.

"What do you think it is?" the perfect woman asked.

"It is a collection of filth and repulsion," he responded.

"No," said two men exploding through the miniature door across the blob. "It is The Heap of Bad Knowledge."

The men were dressed in clothes made from the skins of horny toads and dragged a crying naked wiggle-woman behind them.

"Those who possess bad knowledge will become one with it," they said.

The horny men tossed the screaming woman into the blob. It oozed around her body and sucked her deep within its mass. Hitler watched her writhing inside of the green soup, unable to break free as her flesh was dissolved by the goo.

After watching her for a few seconds Adolf became bored and turned to the men. One of them had a rather impressive handlebar mustache, so Adolf deduced that he was the one in charge.

"Bad Knowledge?" he asked the man with the handlebar mustache. "What is bad about knowledge?"

"The Goddess says that knowledge is evil," he replied.

"Nonsense!" Adolf cried. "Inefficiency and imperfection are evil. Without knowledge, you would be imperfect."

"Do you not agree that this pile of toxic mass is pure evil?" asked the man with the handlebar mustache.

"Yes," Adolf said. "It does have some of the characteristics of evil, but I do not see what it has to do with knowledge."

The lizard-clothed men shifted in their places and said, "The Goddess says this slime pool was once a collection of thoughts that were so intelligent they condensed into matter. And upon looking at its ugliness, She concluded that intelligence is an ugly thing."

"A culture without intelligence is what is ugly," Adolf told them. "This goddess of yours is sorely mistaken."

"You swine!" cried the man with the handlebar mustache. "Who are you to judge the Goddess?"

"I do not know who I am. My memory is in disarray."

The man with the handlebar mustache looked closely at his uniform. "You are Adolf Hitler."

"I am NOT Adolf Hitler. I do not know who Adolf Hitler is, but I assure you he was not two inches high as you can see I am now."

"Then perhaps you are this God person . . ." said the man with the handlebar mustache.

"God is the name of a supreme being and not a human-insect as myself. You should know, you have a goddess. A god is the male version of a goddess. But the God I am speaking of is the only true God. He is perfect, something that I temporarily am not. But I must stress that I will be perfect again one day."

"I don't understand, are you claiming to be a male version of a goddess?" said the man with the handlebar mustache.

"I think your lack of intelligence is causing this confusion," Hitler said. "I am not God nor Adolf Hitler. I am a temporarily flawed perfect man without a name at the present."

"Come," said the man with the handlebar mustache, "We must see the Goddess at once. If we do not gaze upon her every ten minutes we will turn into dust in the cobwebs."

"That is quite impossible," Hitler said. "You must be mistaken on this matter. I agree it is plausible that beings can turn to dust, especially after a very long period of time, but failing to gaze upon a goddess surely would not cause this to happen."

"You sound as if you might possess bad knowledge," said the man with the handlebar mustache. "Do not bring it into our colony or She might banish you into the knowledge slime."

"Do not worry," Hitler said. "Most of my intelligence has either been forgotten or is scrambled in confusion."

The two men took Hitler through a sloping cardboard hallway, the perfect woman following obediently, to a balcony which was once an air vent.

"There she is," said the man with the handlebar mustache as he pointed down a hundred stories to a giant bed.

The Goddess was the corpse of the ghost girl's mother, the corpse that was infested with hundreds of miniature people within the mirror room.

"She is dead," Hitler told them, looking down at the colony of people living within the hollowed out corpse.

"She is not," they said. "She is a skeleton but she is definitely alive in spirit."

"Your culture is an abomination," Hitler told them.

"No, it isn't," cried the man with the handlebar mustache. "Your scrambled thoughts have it wrong. It is the undergoers who have the culture that is an abomination."

"The undergoers?" asked Hitler's perfect woman. "What makes them an abomination?"

"They are evil," said the man with the handlebar mustache. "Ultimate evil."

"They are intelligent, aren't they?" Hitler asked. "I bet you think they are ultimate evil because they are geniuses. Perhaps they are so smart they know how to return my memory and bring me back to normal size!"

"Their culture is an abomination," said the man with

the handlebar mustache.

"Perhaps, but no more than your culture!" Hitler said.

"If you truly feel this way then we must send you to them immediately," said the man with the handlebar mustache. "Otherwise you will offend the Goddess and She will have to banish you to The Heap of Bad Knowledge."

"This will be for the best," Hitler said and the perfect woman agreed.

Without hesitation, the men took them back down the hallway to the same door they came from. However, when it opened it was a different room. This room no longer contained the toxic snot. Now it was filled with concrete statues of angels and a giant hole in the ground.

"What insanity is this?" Adolf cried. "This room contained a pile of toxic snot and now it is filled with concrete statues of angels and a giant hole in the ground!"

The man with the handlebar mustache calmed Hitler and said, "Yes, the size of our living area is so confined that we have to keep many rooms within the same area. You just push a button on the door and *whoosh!* the room becomes another."

"How is that done then?" Adolf asked.

"If we were to possess that kind of knowledge there would be great consequences," said the man with the handlebar mustache. "The undergoers created it a long time ago, when they lived up here with us. Only they know how it works. We only know how to use it and that is enough."

"So we must go down in the hole?" Hitler asked.

"Yes, you'll fall several thousands of meters," he

said.

"Won't that kill us?"

"No, the undergoers created it so that you fall very slowly and will land on your feet."

"How amazing!" Hitler said. "I will love to meet these undergoers. They must be closer to perfect than the usual people of _____ Town."

"They are disgusting, a disease to this world and we wish somebody would cure it of them," said the man with the handlebar mustache.

Hitler frowned at him, then took his perfect woman by the wrist and jumped down the hole.

Mrs. Darkness

They floated for several hours, holding each other and sighing as they fell.

"It is not everyday that I go plummeting into a foreign terrain," young Hitler said to the perfect woman. "This is quite abnormal and mostly unpleasant."

The perfect woman said nothing, squeezing his hand. Her silence made him feel warm and comfortable.

"You know me better than I do," he said to her.

They fell for a few more minutes . . .

"Nobody knows you better than I do," she said.

A few more minutes of falling . . .

"Then who am I?" he asked her. "Tell me of my past."

No response.

A couple meters pass by . . .

"You are Adolf Hitler," she said.

Several more meters . . .

Hitler was beginning to consider the possibility that this perfect woman was not at all real. What she knew about him was only as much as he knew about himself, which was very little. Perhaps she knew even less. The youngish officer at least knew that his name was not really Adolf Hitler.

Or am I? Am I really the one called Hitler? No, Hitler is probably a great man who would never be plummeting into a dark hole as I am. He must be some kind of great king of a man because his name is next to God on my uniform. And I am positive that God is the most perfect being in the universe. So is Hitler the second most perfect? Perhaps. I am not sure. I am just sure that I am not him. But what of this woman? She must be a figment of fantasy. Or perhaps I am living within my subconscious at the moment and this woman is a part of it. A figment of memory. She knows nothing about my history because she is part of my presently faulty brain.

Hitler didn't know what to say to her after that. They just floated in the darkness, invisible to each other. He looked up, searching for the lighted room from where they jumped, there was nothing but darkness above. He looked down and there was no light down that way either, nor to either side of them. Perhaps they were not falling at all. They could just be levitating in midair.

"It does take a long time to fall," Hitler said to the darkness.

"Well, at least we won't get hurt by falling," replied the darkness.

Hitler fell asleep and woke up a few times. Or maybe he was just blinking. Time was not its usual self and things were beginning to get confusing to young Adolf. He dazed in and out of being. The only thing constant was a slight breeze against his uniform and the warm fingers in his hand. He wasn't sure if there was a woman attached to the fingers. There was only darkness.

"Perhaps the bottom has disappeared," said the darkness.

"It is impossible," Adolf said.

As his words finished, their feet tapped gently onto solid ground.

"Now what?" asked the darkness.

"I am not sure," Adolf replied. "We can not see if anything is here or not. The darkness is unending."

"Perhaps these undergoers live in darkness?" asked the darkness.

"That would be absurd," Adolf said. "If they are men of science they would live in culture and not darkness."

"What is culture?" asked the darkness.

"Culture is a civilization pure of imperfection."

"Then perhaps the undergoers are no more. Perhaps they died and we are alone in a dark world."

"I fear your logic, but it might be correct. In that case, we are trapped and lost. We will most surely die."

"We must feel around for food," said the darkness. "Perhaps we can still survive."

The woman patted her hands around on the floor.

"It is not worth surviving in a world of darkness," Adolf said.

The woman continued to search the ground. Adolf did not bother to help.

"Do you remember when we first met?" he asked. Pause.

"Of course," said the darkness.

"How did we meet?"

She did not reply, creeping her hands quickly.

"I found something!" she cried.

"I'm not going to eat anything you found in the dark," he told her.

"It is not food," she said. "It is a lever of some kind."

"Pull it," Adolf said. "Perhaps it will reverse gravity and take us back to the top."

She pulled the lever and light exploded into the room from below.

"A passage!" she said.

The lever had opened a trapdoor in the ground.

"Come on," said the woman as she took the officer towards the world of new light.

Mr. Noseless

They climbed down a ladder made of red and white plastic milkshake straws, descending through puffy pink clouds that were spongy and moist against their bodies. Below the cloudcover there were large trees of blue fungus and spicy needles of cinnamon grass.

"Here we are," said the woman as their feet hit the yellow soil.

It was a whole new world down there. The underground seemed to have its own self-contained atmosphere. Light from an artificial sun shined through the floating pink pillows. The landscape was a clutter of wet, rubbery vegetation. Giant oily mushrooms high above their heads. Sticky puddles of marmalade underneath their feet.

"This place is impure," Adolf said to the perfect woman.

She shrugged.

"We are in nature but it is unnatural," he continued. "This is not a friendly environment."

The perfect woman wasn't listening. She was busy making a dress out of an enormous flower petal.

"We must find civilization as soon as possible.

These undergoers must have a village nearby." Adolf pointed in the direction of the artificial sunlight. "This way. There must be a town this way."

For several hours, they slogged through greasy mushroom forests and yellow powdery spore fields, but civilization was not to be found. Adolf tried his best to keep his uniform clean, wiping away yellow dust with his knuckles. He also tried his best to complain about every little detail he disliked about the underworld.

"Purple grass? Grass is not supposed to be purple. What kind of crazy grass grows purple instead of green? And is that a square rose? Flowers are not supposed to be square. And what is with that tree over there that is growing tennis shoes instead of fruit? Shoes are made in factories, they can not be grown. Why are you putting a pair of them on your feet? I smell something wormy. *Wormy* is not even a real smell. What is the problem with those boulders? They look like a giant marble collection. And why oh why is there a marshmallow waterfall coming out of the hillside?"

"Marshmallow waterfall?" asked the perfect woman.

"Yes, over there," Adolf said, pointing at a river of white goo flowing down the side of the hill up ahead.

"I do not think that is marshmallow," said the woman.

"Well, it is some kind of fluffy white substance," Adolf said. "Perhaps it is not marshmallow, but I would not doubt it to be upon closer inspection."

They moved in for closer inspection. Upon reaching the waterfall, they discovered a strange man. The strange man wore fur clothing that Adolf assumed was made from a mouse. He was sitting by the side of the white river, filling a bowl with the goop from the small waterfall.

The man heard their footsteps and turned to them. Adolf cringed at his appearance. The man didn't have a nose on his face. It must have recently been ripped off by a wild animal, because his face was a bloody mess. The man smiled and waved at them, eating his white soup with a homemade wooden spoon.

As the marshmallow puss entered the man's mouth, Hitler's jaw went slack. He realized the substance was not marshmallow, but some kind of foul smelling lard.

"Why did you eat that?" Adolf said, as if accusing the man of doing something wrong.

"I'm hungry," said the noseless man, still smiling at them.

"It is disgusting," said Adolf.

"Actually, it's pretty good," said the man, raising his big fluffy eyebrows. "I haven't eaten all day."

"Well, stop," Adolf said. "It is disgusting to watch you eat it, especially with that messy wound on your face."

"Very well," said the noseless man. He happily dumped the food in a jar and put it in his backpack. "I'll save it for later."

"Thank you," Adolf said. He was pleased that the noseless man understood how disgusting he was to watch while eating. "Perhaps you can point us in the direction of civilization?"

"Sure thing, pal. I'm headed to _____ City myself."

"_____ City? What are the citizens of _____ City like?"

"Well, if you ask me, they are all quite mad."

"Mad? How terrible! I was under the impression that they would be intelligent people."

"Oh, they are intelligent," said the noseless man. "There are some very, very brilliant minds living there."

"But you said they were insane?"

"Yes, they are insane as well."

"But they can not possibly be intelligent if they are also insane."

"Well, these people are. They are mad, but they are mad geniuses. You know how the greatest geniuses are usually eccentric, right?"

"No," Adolf replied. "That is absurd. A mad man can not possibly be a genius. A genius is one who possesses great intelligence, efficiency, and perfect sanity. Insanity is a great imperfection that geniuses could never possess."

"Well, you will see."

"Perhaps . . ." Adolf was pondering. "They could have *some* intelligence. Do you by any chance think they have the intelligence to return us to natural size?"

"No," said the noseless man. "I was hoping for the same thing, but these people will have nothing of that. Their home is small and they have no intention of leaving it to be big."

"But perhaps they have the knowledge but have never used it?"

"Perhaps," said the noseless man.

They stopped speaking and stared at each other for

a while. Adolf examined a plant with human fingers for thorns. They seemed to be curling at him.

"You haven't seen an imperfect man down here, have you?" Adolf asked the noseless man.

"Imperfect, in what way?" asked the noseless man.

"I am not sure, but he is a disease to this world and I am here to cure it of him."

"Am I your imperfect man?" asked the noseless man. "As you see, my face is missing a nose. Physically, I am quite imperfect."

"I am not sure. I do not remember exactly what the man's imperfection is but I do not think a man with a missing nose is important enough for someone of my stature to be seeking. The one I want has impure genes."

"Well, it is quite possible that your man is down here. The dakar spider shrinks an awful lot of people who normally escape down into this underworld before the spider can get them."

"That is good," young Adolf said. "I will hunt him down and destroy him immediately. But then I must find a way to grow back to normal size so that I can return to my stable healthy perfect lifestyle."

"Then we must keep in touch so that we may find a way to grow back to normal size together."

"Good idea. Although I find your missing nose very unsettling, it would be wise to form an alliance."

"Yes, an alliance."

The perfect woman stewed behind Adolf's shoulder, angered at the idea of sharing company with the noseless man. She snarled at him and gave him dirty looks. Adolf understood her feelings.

"My name is Eyebrows, Roger Eyebrows," he said, holding out his hand.

Adolf did not accept his greeting.

"And you must be Adolf Hitler."

Mr. Roger Eyebrows

"So where is this city?" Adolf asked Roger Eyebrows, as they stepped carefully through the fungus forest.

"Keep walking," replied the noseless man.

So they kept walking for more hours. The landscape changed several times as they walked. It went from a mushroom world into fields of skeleton trees into a desert of abandoned washing machines into a swampland of brown glue until they arrived at their destination.

"Here we are," said the noseless man.

The landscape of red sludge told nothing of civilization.

"Where?" Adolf asked the noseless man.

"All around us," he said.

Adolf looked around to the boundless miles of tar mud.

"There is nothing here," Adolf told him.

"Well, the town is turned off right now. I have to turn it back on to wake it up."

"Turn it on?" Adolf asked. "You can turn an entire city on and off like a light switch?"

"Sure," said the noseless man. "The Golden Eel

invented it. He likes to have complete control over the city, in every possible way."

"You know of the Golden Eel?" Adolf asked him.

"Yes, he is the mayor of the city."

"But I thought he was the mayor of the town above."

"I believe you are mistaken," said the noseless man as he went to a large black snail-shaped rock. He opened up a purple panel on the side and fingered a small switch inside.

Then he turned the city on.

The city exploded into sight: a rushing of spikes and buildings, structures like black cacti, dark and crude as it shrieked out of the mud. Men appeared all around them, walking, talking, working, like they had no idea they just came out of the ground, scurrying by in slime-filthy business suits. Many of them possessed hideous deformities. Some had three eyeballs, some had shark fin heads, lobster hands, demon tails, bubbling frog stomachs, eagle feathers, porcupine hair. Some wore furry suits, others wore black leather with metal spiked collars.

"A whole city of freaks!" Adolf yelled at the city of freaks.

The perfect woman quite agreed.

"Welcome to _____ City," said the noseless man.

Adolf stepped forward onto the tar-brick street, staring up at the burnt rubber skyscrapers, watermills whisper-dangling from balconies, windows without glass, scorpion vines crawling in and out of the structures, giant beetles in the street like autocars. Adolf's face contorted at the sight, so complex and chaotic, alive yet diseased.

Mock-people running around in alien ways, *imperfect* people. But these were not just like the imperfect-gened human beings that Adolf tracked down for a living. These creatures could hardly be considered human beings at all. They should be called half-humans. Or less-humans. Or anti-humans. Or just freaks. Or animals that should be put on chains.

"Do you have a leash for her?" the noseless man asked.

"A leash?" Adolf asked.

The noseless man pointed to the perfect woman. "She needs a leash in the city. And tags. It's the law."

"Women need to be leashed?" Adolf asked. "What a curious law . . ."

"You're joking," the perfect woman said, but Adolf held his hand out to stop her from speaking.

"This is quite barbaric," Adolf said. "You let all these strange creatures roam free, yet my utterly perfect partner must be chained."

"It's the law," said Roger Eyebrows.

Adolf thought about it. "Very well. I will not break the law. This city might be an abominable disease, but it is my only hope for our return to the normal world."

"I don't see any other women on leashes," said the perfect woman and Adolf hushed her again with his hand.

"You must register her at the pet shop," said the noseless man.

"Pet shop?" cried the woman.

"Take us to the pet shop then," Adolf told the noseless man.

"Actually, I am too busy to take you anywhere. It is

the red building on the corner."

"Busy?" Adolf asked.

"I must prepare for the festivities tonight."

"I thought we were a team?"

"A team?" asked the noseless man. "Why would we be a team?"

"Because both of us are seeking a way to return to the surface."

"Surface?" asked the noseless man. "I don't understand you."

"We need to find a way to get back to normal-size."

"Normal-size? We *are* normal-sized. You are quite an unusual man. What did you call yourself again?"

"I do not call myself anything," Adolf said.

"Ah, yes," he said, looking at the uniform. "I remember now. You are Adolf Hitler."

Mr. Song

The cricket-people hopped and craned and vibrated at them as they crossed the street to the pet shop.

"Madness!" Adolf exclaimed, as they stepped into the stone pet shop.

"Madness," mimicked a parrot in the corner.

The parrot had peach-colored feathers with the head and breasts of a human woman.

The young Adolf examined all the pets in the shop. Every one of them seemed to be some kind of animal/woman mutation. There was a woman/cat with fur and claws scratching at a dead woman/mouse. There was a woman/goldfish in a fishbowl, breathing through gills on her slender white neck. There was a woman with floppy ears and a wet nose.

The owner of the pet shop stared proudly at his inventory, rubbing the black and white hairs on his chin. Adolf stepped closer to him, discovering that the man had a familiar face. It was Mr. Wheel, the old inn keeper.

"Mr. Wheel?" Adolf asked.

"Who?" asked the old man.

"Are you not Mr. Wheel from above?"

"I am Mr. Song," said the pet shop owner. "I am the pet shop owner."

"I am mistaken then," Adolf said. "You look exactly like a man named Mr. Wheel. Perhaps it is because you are both old. I am not used to old people. You all look alike."

Mr. Song crook-grinned, then chuckled. "Well, that is the most impolite greeting I've ever heard. Who might you be?"

"I am not Adolf Hitler," Adolf told him. "We are looking for a way for this woman to walk about this town lawfully."

"You'll need a license," said Mr. Song. "No worries. Let me just fill out this form . . ."

Mr. Song took a square orange piece of paper out of a white piano in the center of the room. He sat down at the piano and used it as a desk.

"Now," said Mr. Song. "What is your lady's name?"

Adolf thought hard about it, but he did not know the answer to the question. He could not remember her name. Looking at the woman for help, she dodged his eyes as if she did not know herself.

"She is . . ." Adolf just picked a word off the top of his head. "Gon . . . gonna . . ."

"Gona?" Mr. Song wrote it down.

"What was your marriage date?"

Adolf's eyes shriveled.

"Marriage date?" he exclaimed. "We were never married."

"Never married? Well, I can't license a stray woman to you. You'll have to marry her immediately or else I'll be forced to put her to sleep."

Adolf's eyes met the woman's. Her eyebrows were twitching in a panic.

Marriage? Well, I could be engaged to this woman already in the normal world. Possibly marrying her would not make any difference and would save her from death. Besides, she is a part of what I have lost and she might be my only hope of getting my memory back.

"Okay, we will get married," Adolf said.

"You have until tonight then," said Mr. Song. "After that, she must either be licensed or put to sleep."

"I will make sure we are married," Adolf said. "Where is the place to perform the marriage ritual?"

"At the ceremony tonight."

"What is this ceremony?"

"It is a celebration of the Golden Eel, our emperor."

"Emperor? I heard his title was mayor."

"No, the Golden Eel is our emperor."

"Is there a Mrs. Neat in Town?" Adolf asked. "I have been told a woman named Mrs. Neat can help me find what I am looking for."

"What are you looking for?" asked Mr. Song.

"I am looking for an imperfect man. I am not sure what he looks like, but I have a picture in my briefcase that knows. Mrs. Neat should know where my briefcase is and where I can find this man. However, I doubt my briefcase is in this town. It is possible, however, that Mrs. Neat is here. And perhaps the imperfect man."

"Well, you've come to the right place to find a woman," said Mr. Song. "I have a record of all the women in town and which owner they are attached to."

Mr. Song opened a large book of scribble-words. Adolf tried to read them, but they didn't seem to be words from a real language.

"Ah, here is Mrs. Neat," said Mr. Song.

Adolf looked closely at the nonsense words and could not find any pattern. The words seemed to move, as if they were melting off of the page.

"She belongs to the high priest," said Mr. Song.

"Are you sure?" I asked.

"Yes, the high priest. He lives in the tin house under the bridge."

"Where is the bridge?"

"You'll find it," said Mr. Song. "You can't miss the bridge."

Mr. Bartender

Walking down the street in search of a bridge, Gona held Adolf's hand tight, attempting to appear leashed to him. The natives shuffle-darted across their path like crazed locusts. They were all men. No women at all. The women must have been left at the men's homes, in cages.

Every mutated anti-human that passed made Adolf sick to his stomach. They jumped in and out of the street without any pattern or direction, bobbling rapidly, as if they moved for the sake of moving and didn't really have any place to go. Watching them made Adolf dizzy. He dropped his sight to his feet, holding a hand in front of his eyes, breathing deep.

"What is wrong?" the woman asked him softly.

He looked into her eyes to calm himself. She smiled and it warmed his heart.

"Let us rest awhile," Adolf said to her.

She nodded and they entered the nearest tavern, one with a melting-rubber roof and railroad walkways. She sat him down in a corner table away from the room's occupants, which were three beetle-men in a moldy center table cheering to themselves and mumbling foreign words.

"This place is driving me to craziness, Gona," his face was turning purple. "I have to leave before it takes me over and makes me imperfect."

"Do not worry," Gona said. "Tonight we will be married and everything will be fine. We will be so happy none of this will matter."

She smiled and held her warm hand on his thumping chest.

A shiver went up his spine.

"The people here are supposed to be genius, but I see no genius in these monstrosities. I see more imperfection than my eyes can handle."

"They may be imperfect, but they are still human beings."

"Nonsense," Adolf said, clenching a fist. "Human beings strive to be efficient and have control over their surroundings. Here, I am out of control. My surroundings drive me into craziness."

"You will get used to it eventually."

"That is what I am afraid of. Once I become unaffected by this chaos, I will be a part of it. I will be one of these monstrosities, absurd and out of control. I will become ugly. The dirt on my skin will be my uniform. A grotesque eel will be my god."

"You talk too much about things," Gona said. "Why always talk so much?"

"I am just talking because it is important."

"I bet you even talk when nobody is around."

"Perhaps I do."

"I bet you talk to strange people you meet in the street."

"I only speak when speaking is important and right now it is important. I need to get myself together so that I can find the bridge and then go under the bridge to find the high priest's house, so I can speak with Mrs. Neat, so I can find my briefcase, so I can look at a photograph, so I can find the imperfect man, so I can complete my mission, so I can figure out a way to grow back to normal size, so I can go home."

"Talking, talking, talking," said the perfect woman.

Adolf looked around the tavern for someone to speak to besides his future pet wife. There weren't any customers other than the beetle-men who didn't look worthy of conversation to Adolf. He held his still-dizzy eyes in stare and focused in on the bartender. Adolf recognized who he was. He was the same bartender from before, in _____ Town. The only man who seemed slightly normal. Adolf stood, leaving Gona in her chair. The bartender recognized him immediately.

"Adolf Hitler," he said. "I see you're still in town."

"But I am not still in town. This is _____ City, not _____ Town."

"Yes, but this is the same bar. The Golden Eel decided to save money by using the same bar in both towns."

"But that's impossible. This building we are in must be only a few feet large. How can cockroach people and normal-sized human beings share the same bar?"

"Easy. The door to this bar has shrinking and enlarging technology. People from _____ City grow larger when they walk through the door and people from _____ Town shrink. The bar is actually an in-between size."

"So you are saying I can grow to normal size if I go through the door to _____ Town?"

"No," said the bartender. "Exiting through the door returns you to the size you entered as. You can't choose which size you wish to be."

"But if you have the technology to enlarge a human being, surely there is a way to return me to my normal size."

"You'll have to speak to The Golden Eel, Mr. Hitler. I am not skilled in the ways of science."

"Where is The Golden Eel?" Adolf asked him.

"He lives in _____ Castle, across the bridge."

"Oh, does he?" Adolf cried. "I shall go see him immediately. Where is this bridge?"

"Everyone knows of the bridge," he said.

"Well, I do not," Adolf said. "Can you please give me directions?"

"Just keep walking the street. I understand the bridge is at the end of it."

"Are you sure?"

"No, that is just what I've heard. I serve drinks to the people of _____ City, but I have never actually been there."

"Well, thank you for your information, Mr. Bartender. Can I please get a sherry? Normally, I prefer sobriety over intoxication but I need something to calm me down."

"Sure," said the bartender. "But you must leave with it."

"Why is that?" Adolf asked.

"Pets are not allowed," he said, pointing at Gona.

"This is a decent establishment I run. Customers do not want to see hair and fleas all over the tables and chairs."

"That is absurd, but I will respect your authority."

"Dirty creatures, women are. You should put her to sleep directly after she gives you her first litter."

"The people are so cruel here."

Adolf drank the gray lawn-flavored fluid that wasn't sherry after the bartender slid it across the counter to him. He cringed at the bartender and left without paying, grabbing Gona angrily as if she was doing something wrong, as if she was the one to blame for being a dirty animal.

As they left the pub, Adolf noticed the streets had been emptied. No chaos, no clutter, no mutated people hopping around. Just Hitler and his fiancé walking among the soggy skeletal buildings.

"Where did they all go?" they asked the silence.

A breeze combined with rusty metal answered, "Gone to prepare for tonight's festivities . . ."

They stepped crackly down the street, trying to ignore the sickness that surrounded them. The road stretched for miles, without any sign of side streets. An entire city in one strip. Hours seemed to pass. Their limbs grew tired.

"It seems to take half a day to go from one end of the city to the other," Adolf told Gona. "Their setup is very illogical. They never cease to disgust me."

"Yes," Gona said. "They designed their entire civilization to irritate you."

Adolf's face wrinkled crude at her and she smiled. Eventually, the road came to an end and The Bridge came to a beginning: a giant wooden extension shaped like a dragonfly, stretching even farther into the distance, the end too far to see.

Somewhere out there must be _____ Castle, where lives the Golden Eel, Adolf thought.

"We have to go under the bridge," Adolf told Gona.

"I know," Gona replied.

"That is where the high priest lives," Adolf told Gona.

Gona nodded.

"I'm going to find him," Adolf told Gona.

Gona nodded.

"I'm going to find a way home."

Gona nodded.

Mrs. Neat

The house was not on the ground as Adolf had imagined. There didn't seem to even be any ground under the bridge, just a swirl of colors that could have been clouds or possibly a distorted landscape far below. So the high priest's house wasn't on the ground, it was in the sky — hanging from the bridge by a string. They walked halfway down the dragonfly's back to a hole that led down to the house's roof, swaying in the breeze.

"It seems deserted," young Adolf told Gona, shivering.

She stared off into the colorful gases.

"Do you want to stay up here?" Adolf asked her.

Her mind was in a spindle.

"Stay here," he ordered.

She stroked her hair.

Hitler climbed down the string to stand awkwardly on the rocking tin house. He stood as steadily as he could but his brain was getting dizzy again, this time from the swirling colors in the sky. The colors came from what looked to be clouds splattered with different colors of paint. The god of this world was not as good an artist as

Hitler's God.

A manhole was beneath his feet. A salty smell rose from the room as he opened the manhole cover and dropped down inside the dangling house.

The smell attacked his nostrils: a strong, mind-melting sea salt smell. Hitler's eyes watered at its intensity. He had to hold his wrist against his nose as he looked around. The room was small and overpopulated with metal furniture covered in tar and filmy fluids.

"Is anybody here?" Hitler called. "Mrs. Neat, perhaps?"

He stepped into the next room, another cluttered mess of black soupy chairs and dressers, calling for Mrs. Neat, keeping his nose from becoming salty.

Adolf heard breathing and tapping noises ahead as he stepped around a corner into a new room.

"Ah, Mr. Hitler," said a voice as he entered the room. "Glad you could make it."

Hitler turned around to find Roger Elbows, the noseless man who brought them to _____ City. He was standing over a black stringy trunk, pouring salt on slugs.

"Are you the high priest?" Adolf asked the noseless man.

"Yes," said the noseless man. "Didn't I tell you? That is why I had to rush away so soon. The high priest is the most essential character in the ceremony tonight. Oh, where is your woman? Did you have her put to sleep?"

"No, she is outside."

"I wouldn't leave her out there by herself for too long. Someone might impound her or steal her, or she might run away."

"I doubt she would run away," Adolf said.

"Oh, you have her trained that well, do you?" asked the noseless man.

"She has only me."

The noseless man barked a laugh and sprinkled more salt on his collection of slugs.

"So what did you come here for, Mr. Hitler?"

"I was told Mrs. Neat resides here. I'm in need of her help."

"Neat?" He chuckled again. "You've come to talk to her?"

"Yes," Adolf said. "The bartender told me she could help me find my briefcase so I can find the imperfect man."

"Well, I don't know about that, but you're welcome to talk to her if you wish."

"Yes, please," Adolf said. "It is vital to national security."

The noseless man chewed on his tongue and led Adolf into another room with a window and velvet curtains that flowed to the ground and across the floor and up another wall and across half the ceiling. A large turtle aquarium centered the room.

"I'll be in the next room if you need me," said the noseless man. "My work is never done."

Adolf was alone in the room. There was no sign of Mrs. Neat.

"Mrs. Neat?" But there wasn't an answer.

The sky outside the window was a gentle swirl of violet and it seemed to flash with sideways lightning. Adolf wondered if it was raining. He wondered if Gona was soaking or becoming sick out there.

He stepped to the aquarium. Inside of the aquarium there was a turtle. There was something wrong with it. The shell of the turtle was not shaped as they normally are. This turtle's shell was different, deformed. It did resemble a turtle shell in color and pattern, but its shape was that of a racecar, with wheels and all.

"Mrs. Neat?" Adolf called again, tapping on the racecar shell.

She must have been asleep. He tapped again and her human head poked out . . . a wrinkled tiny bald human head. And her human feet came out of the racecar wheels and she yawned.

"Are you Mrs. Neat?" Adolf asked her.

She pecked at crickets and bologna.

"Mrs. Neat?"

The house rocked back and forth, creating nausea in the pit of Adolf's belly.

"I am Mrs. Neat," said the turtle, chewing on earwigs and a pear. Her shriveled papier-mâché limbs worm-wriggled. "Have you come to hear my stories?"

"I have come for another reason," Adolf said to the turtle.

"I have lived for such a long time. I have so many stories to tell."

"I apologize for my impatience, Mrs. Neat, but I am on a mission of utmost importance and have not the time nor the need for stories." Spidery green patterns doll-crept across the sky and stuttered his voice. "I am in search of a man who is a threat to mankind. An imperfect man."

"Imperfect?" asked the turtle. "In what way?"

"I am not sure," Adolf said. "I can not remember his face, but it is imperfect. He is a disease and I am here to cure society of him. He has led me into this world of ill-genes and anti-normality. I have been told you are the one to help me."

The turtle squirted gray mucus on her chipped-bark floor.

"I am only a turtle," said the turtle. "Humans rarely cross my path. Even if I have seen the man you seek, defining him as *imperfect* does not give me an image him. All humans are imperfect. You must give me a visual description and maybe I have seen him."

Adolf crossed his eyes. "I have a photo of this man in my briefcase but I can not find this briefcase."

The turtle stopped and soaked in the window light, closing her eyes tight.

"It probably went to the place where things go," she said.

"Where do things go?" Adolf asked the turtle.

"All things have life. Even the ones you came to believe are not animated. Sometimes when you are not looking, your things will get up and go off on their own journey. They sometimes go to a land of *things*, where all unanimated objects walk freely. Your briefcase might have found a home there."

"Where is this place of alive things?" he asked the turtle.

"I am only a turtle," answered the turtle. "I do not know these things. You should ask the Golden Eel. He knows many things."

"I find your answer a bit hopeful," he said to the turtle, "yet hideously preposterous. The idea of a land where objects have life is even more absurd than the racecar-shaped shell on your back. It is more absurd than your high priest without a nose. It is more absurd than this house held by a string."

"Do you have a place to stay?" asked the turtle.

"No, I have just arrived in _____ City. I have not made temporary living arrangements as of yet. Though it might be important to find a place since I am marrying Gona this evening."

"You must stay here in the high priest's home as our guests."

"That is a very kind offer," Adolf said to the turtle, "but I feel very uncomfortable in this structure. I would not even allow Gona to come down here with me."

"You don't have to worry. It is safer here than in the city."

"Why is it not safe in the city?"

"People disappear at night," said the turtle. "They are mysteriously taken away. Nobody is sure why they are taken or what is taking them. No, the city is not a safe place at all."

"This place is so unorganized that I am not surprised such things take place," Adolf said to the turtle. "You have no control over your people or environment or even yourselves. Deaths and disappearances are bound to occur in such a situation."

"Your heart does not speak these words," said the turtle. "Just your mouth."

"You are a confused little creature," he said to the

turtle.

"Nobody else will give you a place to stay, Mr. Hitler. This is your only home unless you want to risk disappearing. Think of your wife if you will not think of yourself."

"She is not yet my wife," he told the turtle.

They paused, staring at the light darkening through the window, pink melting into a hot blood red.

"You will stay here, Adolf Hitler," said the turtle.

"I am *not* Adolf Hitler," he said to the turtle.

"You will stay here, Mr. Hitler," she hissed, like a scary evil doll.

Father Noseless

Leaving Mrs. Neat's room, Adolf's feet slipped out from under him and he collapsed into a puddle of black goo, soaking his elbows and pants with melted slugs.

"Oh, Mr. Hitler!" cried the noseless high priest, entering the room to help him up from the soupy floor. "You must get out of that uniform and into something clean."

"I have nothing clean," Adolf said. "And your clothes are too sickly for me to wear."

"Oh, but you must," said the noseless high priest. "You can not wear any black clothing at the wedding ceremony. It is bad luck."

"Only primitives believe in luck," Adolf said to the noseless high priest.

"Strange," said the noseless high priest. "I was taught that only primitives do not believe in luck. Please, take off your clothes."

Adolf groaned at him. "Fine."

"Here, wear this," said the noseless man, handing Adolf a yellow robe. "It will suit you much better than that awful uniform."

"Should my woman wear new clothes?" Adolf asked the noseless man.

"Women do not wear clothes in the ceremony," he replied.

"A dignified woman would not expose her natural self to the public," Adolf told the noseless man.

"I find it quite ridiculous for a man of your age to treat your woman as if she is another human being."

"She is another human being," Adolf told him.

The noseless man exploded into chuckles. "Don't go telling anyone else that."

Adolf slipped the robe over his mucky uniform and tied it together. The priest's facial expression told him that he didn't approve of keeping the uniform on underneath the robe, but he didn't argue.

"Will it begin soon?" Adolf asked.

"Yes," the priest's mood switched to dreary. "I can feel the night approaching."

Climbing up a ladder out of the manhole of the high priest's home, the atmosphere struck Adolf with fierce colors of blood red storming down on them with streaks of yellow and black. Even the wind was dark red as it attacked his hair.

"What is wrong with the sky?" Adolf asked the noseless man, yelling over the loud wind.

"The night is bleeding in," said the noseless man.

The tin house rocked violently in the wind as they climbed the string up to the dragonfly/bridge. Gona was at the top, gazing into the void below, her figure wasping in the red wind, clothes fire-flickering.

"Gona," Adolf called to her, but she did not turn

around. "It is time."

"Women do not obey when you treat them as equals," said the noseless man.

"Come, Gona," Adolf called.

She turned to Hitler, her face dazed and distant.

The noseless man went to her. "Let's go, woman!"

Gona went to Hitler's side and smiled at him, touching her hand to his chin. Then they went back to town.

Walking across the giant crispy dragonfly was like walking in a dream. The colors shifted in and out of them, the ground distorted as his feet touched them.

"I am feeling odd," Adolf told the noseless man high priest.

"Of course you do," said the noseless high priest. "The atmosphere is artificial, made from chemicals. The night is made out of chemicals that are intoxicating when breathed."

"You mean I have been drugged against my will?" asked Adolf Hitler.

"The only way to stop the intoxication is to stop breathing," said the noseless high priest.

"Who created this atmosphere?" Adolf asked the noseless high priest.

"The emperor, of course, The Golden Eel. He feels having a night is worth putting up with the side effects."

"His eccentricity does not surprise me, but I do hate feeling out of control."

Upon entering the city, Adolf felt like he was breathing though his pores, through his eyeballs, through the ears, the toenails, the fingertips, through hairs, through

Adolf in Wonderland

his private parts, breathing as if he was a collection of lungs molded into human form.

The town seemed different at night. The buildings were coated in a thick tar substance similar to the melted slug goo covering his uniform. They emitted an odor that was carried by the red wind down the road to assault Adolf's senses.

"We must hurry," said the noseless high priest. "People disappear at night."

They left the road halfway into the soggy city and entered the crop fields.

A crowd of robed men were gathered at the edge of the fields, many in yellow robes identical to Hitler's, some in red and white. The crowd gazed silently at them as if they were the spotlight of the ceremony.

"Stand over there," said the noseless high priest, pointing to a line of yellow-robed men.

Adolf took his place at the end of the line. Gona did not follow. The noseless high priest whispered something in her ear, almost kissing it and caressing her lobe with the gory noseless region of his face. Then he stripped her of her clothes, exposing her perfect nudity to the crowd of slobbering mutants. He took her by the hand and led her through some tall squirrel bushes and disappeared out of sight.

When the noseless man returned, he was alone. His sleeves were covered in mud and his hands were folded into a knot. Next to Adolf, a large warthog man was snorting and licking his snotty nostrils with his thick gray tongue. His odor was not unlike the diarrhea of a diseased ostrich. On the other side of Adolf was a black hairy creature that resembled a cross between an obese tarantula and a giant deformed vagina with five cat tails for arms. Both were horrible putrid creatures that Adolf believed should not be permitted to stand within a mile of his presence, but Adolf decided to inch his way closer to the warthog man because he at least somewhat resembled a human being. Adolf turned slightly, so he could put his backside to the tarantulagina. The warthog man noticed Adolf leaning into him and grunted. Before he had the chance to use his better judgment, Adolf opened his mouth to speak to him.

"How does this work?" Adolf asked the warthog man.

The warthog man grunted.

"What happens? What are we supposed to do?"

The warthog man grunted.

"This whole situation is ludicrous," he said to the warthog man.

"It is an abomination," grunted the warthog man.

"Yes!" Adolf cried to the warthog man. "I agree! It is an abomination!"

Adolf smiled and looked up at the beastly creature. He grunted and licked his snotty nostrils with his thick gray tongue.

At that moment, the dizziness hit Adolf hard. He could feel rough/vibrating textures in the air when he breathed. The people around him were becoming pixilated. The smell of the creatures caused his brain to itch and tickle. There was a flame that danced through the air like a lava fairy.

Then Adolf shook his head and sobered a bit. The fire was from a torch the noseless high priest carried with him as he approached the crowd of yellow-robed men. There was silence around him. The ceremony was about to begin . . .

"My grooms," said the noseless man, "today you are about to commit to the trial called marriage. On behalf of all the citizens of _____ City, we salute you for this sacrifice. As disgusting as it may be, marriage is important to our civilization. Without marriage there would be no way to propagate our species. You are heroes, every one of you. Your suffering will ensure a future for our people. As tradition dictates, we recommend you put your woman to sleep after she gives her first litter. With our current technology, women are no longer required during the infancy stages after birth and it would only be cruel to the children to keep the woman around. As we know, children often become attached to their mothers because they don't know any better. This is something that you do not want to happen. So, please, make sure to terminate the woman as soon as she gives birth."

The noseless high priest signaled to a group of red-robed lobster-men who approached the line with boxes of pet collars.

"This is how the ceremony will go," continued the noseless high priest. "You will each be given a collar. It is your wedding ring. As soon as you put the wedding ring on your woman, you will be locked into the bonds of marriage. But first, you must find your woman. All of the brides have been hidden in the field. As soon as you find your wife, you will put your wedding ring around her neck and then mate with her. There will be no going back then. After you mate, by law, you must remain married to your woman until she gives birth at least once. If your woman proves to be unable to give birth, you can exchange your wife for a new one."

Adolf was handed a collar. It was a bit large for Gona. It seemed to have been made for a horse. The warthog man next to him was equally perplexed by the size of his collar. His seemed to be made for a woman the size of a cat.

"Following the ceremony," continued the noseless high priest, "there will be a feast and a celebration to honor you brave men. As you all know, it is tradition that one of the brides be served as the main course of the feast. This dinner bride, as we call her, will be the woman who is married last. The groom of the dinner bride will be dishonored and sent home. So if you do not want to be known as a traitor and a coward, you better make sure you aren't the last man to find your wife."

Adolf's heart was pumping quickly. His hands were quivering. He couldn't believe what the ugly priest had said.

Did he say that they would eat the loser's wife? Does that mean that Gona, the most perfect woman in the world, could be eaten by these atrocious creatures if I find her last?

As Adolf's heart pumped, his blood rushed through his body, and he could feel effects of the drug intensifying. His vision was becoming blurry. The warthog man next to him made some noises into his ear but Adolf wasn't sure if he was snorting or trying to tell him something.

How am I going to be able to find Gona in my current state?

"After this torch hits the ground," continued the noseless high priest. "You may begin the hunt."

The fire of the torch was laughing at Adolf as the priest raised it over his head.

"Begin," said the noseless high priest.

Adolf scowled at the fire as it laughed and mocked. He couldn't understand what it was saying, but its crackling words angered him.

After a few minutes, Adolf realized the torch was already on the ground and the other grooms were running off in other directions. He was just standing there, alone with the priests, staring at the torch on the ground.

Mrs. Pig

Adolf ran off after the other grooms into the field. His steps were like purple ooze. He seemed to be in slow motion. The peripherals of his eyes were crackling with white light. Wandering aimlessly through the yellow fungus fields, he could barely see anything but jittery textures in front of him.

The other grooms seemed to find their brides quickly. Adolf passed several mutant couples making love in the drippy bushes or behind the mossy rocks. Everywhere he stepped there were grooms with their wives, staring at him and giggling to themselves.

Or are they not real? Hallucinations, maybe? If this artificial night induces this disgusting mind-scattering state then why do I seem to be the only one effected? Have they all grown used to it? Maybe their rotten minds are so naturally disturbed that they can not tell the difference between this and normality.

Adolf kept searching for what seemed like an hour. He couldn't find any bride without a groom let alone Gona. He had lost. Surely, his Gona was going to be killed by these creatures. And his mind was so spiky-sick that there

Adolf in Wonderland

was nothing he could do about it.

Out of pyramid patterns, the warthog man emerged and slammed into him. They fell over each other and squished into the slimy yellow mold on the ground.

"Where is my woman?" Adolf thought the warthog man said.

His brain was having a difficult time comprehending language.

"I do not know," Adolf might have said. "What does she look like?"

"A pig," Adolf thought the warthog man said.

"Have you seen my wife?" Adolf might have asked the warthog man.

"What does she look like?" Adolf thought the warthog man asked him.

"She looks perfect."

Adolf then realized that he still had a chance. This mutant had not found his mutant wife yet, so he was not yet the last groom to find his wife. He wondered if they were the last two left, competing for second to last place. As long as the warthog man didn't find his wife first, Adolf could save Gona.

The look on the warthog man's face told the young Hitler that he was thinking the same thing. Before the warthog could react, Adolf snatched the collar from his hand and tossed it over his shoulder into a pool of mud. His face cartoonishly stretched into a shrieking thunder cloud and knocked Adolf to the ground.

The warthog man, in return, took the collar away from Adolf and tossed it over a purple hedge before diving into the mud to retrieve his. Snorting and squealing noises from behind as Adolf darted after his collar, jumping over the hedge into the lap of a giant ball of blubber.

It wasn't a ball of blubber. It was a naked woman. A pig woman. She had caught Adolf's collar as it fell over the hedge and was thanking the heavens as the youngish man landed on her. She was waiting for Adolf to put the collar on her, kissing his neck with her wet snout, rubbing her six breasts against his shoulder. She was enormous. Twice Gona's size. Maybe even larger than the warthog man who obviously was supposed to be her groom.

Adolf took the collar away from the pig woman and she raised her neck so that he could put it on, but Adolf crawled off of her. Before he could sneak away, she lunged at him with all of her greasy blubber strength.

"Please, please," Adolf thought the pig woman cried. "I don't want to die."

"Get off of me, you enormous blob!" Adolf might have told the pig woman.

"Pleeeease . . ." The pig woman sobbed into his yellow robe. "I'll be a good wife. I will give you lots of children. Don't let them eat me. Please, don't let me die."

Her sow eyes widened at Adolf. They watered down her cheeks onto his chest. Perhaps it was because of the drugs, but Adolf was beginning to feel sorry for her. She was a horribly disgusting creature, but perhaps she didn't deserve to die.

"Okay," Adolf thought he told the pig woman. "I will put the collar on you."

The pig woman's mouth opened wide with excitement. She snuggled him against her blubbery breasts and licked him with her thick rancid tongue. After she got off of him, she leaned in, tilted her head, and closed her eyes as Adolf opened the collar around her throat. But he didn't put it on her. He dropped it. And before she could hear the collar hit the ground, Adolf wrapped his arm around her throat and broke her deformed neck.

Her enormous body went limp. Adolf retrieved his wedding ring, covered her with purple vegetation, and moved on. As he left, he could hear the warthog man crying, desperately trying to find his collar in the mud.

Gona was safe now. The warthog man would come in last and the pig woman would be dinner for these freaks. All Adolf had to do was find his perfect woman.

Adolf didn't find her, though. She found him. Adolf was wandering through a forest of crab-legs when she came up from behind and wrapped her slender arms around him. She tilted him down and kissed him deeply. He put the collar around her neck and she pulled him into a bed of fuzzy moss. As they made love, the drugs in Hitler's system intensified and everything around him became a twisty blur. His senses melted together. He could smell the warmth of her skin. He could taste her sweat through his fingertips.

As Adolf came, his brain turned into a metallic liquid that rushed through his lungs and dripped out of his nipples into Gona's mouth. His thoughts drifted down her throat as their bodies pressed together as tight as they could.

PART THREE
The Queen of Eels

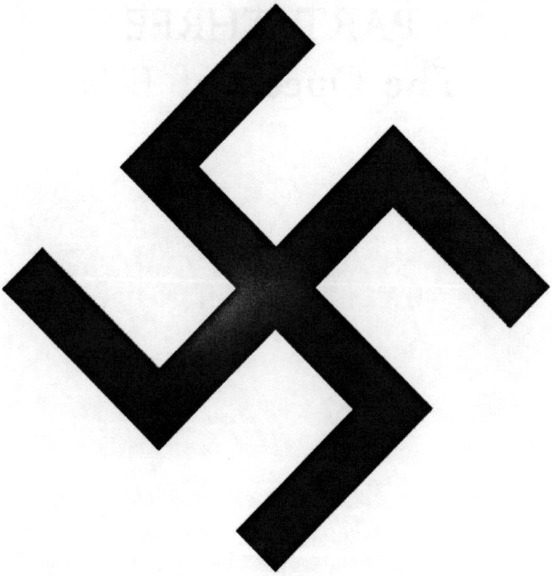

Mr. and Mrs. Hitler

It seemed to young Adolf Hitler that he had been sleeping for decades. He awoke to his new wife's face surrounded by black hairy blankets. He was in a bed somewhere. The lighting was dim. Her eyes were open, staring at her husband, as if she had been lying there waiting for him to wake up.

"You slept long," she said.

His head was pounding, almost like a hangover. It was probably caused by the drug in the artificial atmosphere. Adolf pulled back the blankets and looked around the room. It was very small, like a closet. Everything was metal and painted black. There was only enough room for a small bed and a toilet. Adolf separated his naked body from Gona's and stood up. She was also nude, except for her wedding collar. The room rocked gently as he urinated into the pot. The motion made him nauseous. He could tell that they were in the noseless high priest's house, dangling from the bridge. The bottom of the toilet bowl was just a hole that led into the great abyss below.

"I have a confession to make," Gona said.

Adolf crawled back into bed. When he touched

Gona's flesh, it was cold. Like the temperature of a corpse.

"I'm sorry, but I was lying to you . . ." Gona said.

Adolf pulled away from her flesh. It was unnaturally cold.

Her face changed. A white form reached out of her body to touch him.

"It's really me, Elsie," said the white form.

It was Mr. Wheel's daughter, the ghost girl. She was inside of Adolf's perfect woman.

"What treachery is this?" Adolf asked the ghost girl.

"I wanted to be with you and knew this was the only way you'd love me back."

Adolf's mouth widened with shock.

"But we're married now," she said. "It's important for married people to be honest with each other if they want to make a marriage work."

She held him. Adolf shivered within her death arms, trying to contain four angry tears.

Mrs. Mantimeleon

Adolf pushed the ghost girl away from him and looked for a sign of Gona. Behind Elsie, on the bed, there was a black creature where Gona had been lying. It was a large woman-creature with skin like a cockroach shell.

"What is that?" Adolf exclaimed to the ghost girl, leaping into the far corner of the room.

Elsie stood and approached him, raising her arms to calm him down.

"In order to change into your perfect woman, I had to possess a mantimeleon. It is a creature that is somewhat a cross between a praying mantis and a chameleon."

Adolf looked down at the sleeping creature. It was very much like a woman-shaped praying mantis, but the size of a gorilla with patches of long black hair.

"It is a monstrosity!" Adolf said to the ghost girl.

"It is safe, for now," said the ghost girl. "It is asleep."

"It is an abomination!" Adolf said to the ghost girl.

"But when it is awake it will be a danger," said the ghost girl. "Humans are one of the major food sources of mantimeleons, next to wild deer, cattle, and big dogs. They have the ability to alter their appearance to look like their prey's perfect mate."

"It is an outrageous spectacle of disgustion!" Adolf said to the ghost girl.

"They are able to lure their prey, seduce them into letting down their guard, then they kill and eat them. I decided to possess one so that I could look like your perfect mate."

"You could never be my perfect mate!" Adolf said.

"But in the mantimeleon I look like your perfect mate," said the ghost girl.

"I would never mate with you," Adolf said.

"We mated last night," said the ghost girl.

"But you are a ghost girl," Adolf said to the ghost girl. "We can not truly mate. Your dead womb could never produce my offspring."

"Yeah," Elsie said softly, trying not to frown. "In my ghost form, I could not. But in that body I can. In fact, we already have."

"I mated with that thing!" Adolf said.

"I'll show you," said the ghost girl.

She went to the door and opened it, letting in two black creatures.

"Daddy!" the creatures screamed, running into the room at him.

Adolf shrieked and jumped on top of the toilet lid. "What the hell are those?"

"Daddy, daddy," cried the creatures, swarming around the toilet seat.

They tried to hug his legs but he kicked at their heads with the heel of his foot.

"They are your children," said the ghost girl.

"Impossible!" Adolf said. "This is a terrible trick! This whole place is a terrible trick!"

"I didn't know mantimeleons could mate with humans," she said, "but I gave birth twice last night for both times we made love."

"We made love twice?"

"Once at the ceremony and once after the festivities."

"What festivities?" Adolf said, cringing as one of the creatures snuggled its cheek against his ankle.

"You weren't really conscious for the festivities. You wouldn't even eat any of the roasted pig."

Adolf tossed a blanket over their black heads and charged out of the room, slamming the door behind him and holding it shut.

The ghost girl walked through the wall and continued speaking to him. "After mating, mantimeleons give birth within just a few hours. I went through two pregnancies last night and gave birth twice, while you were asleep. Baby mantimeleons grow fast. It should take them only a few days for them to grow to adulthood."

She watched Adolf as he desperately held the door closed to keep the creatures inside.

"Let them out," she said. "They are our children."

"They aren't your children," Adolf said. "They are that creature's children."

The woman wrapped her cold hands around his wrists.

"I will still love them as if they were my own," said the ghost girl.

Mrs. Stick and Mr. Mohawk

After an hour, Elsie was able to calm Adolf down enough to let the children into the room.

"Hi, daddy," said the male child as he passed him to go into the kitchen.

"I love you, daddy," said the female child with her plump hairy face.

They were no longer interested in attacking Adolf with their love. They were only interested in breakfast.

"Aren't they adorable?" Elsie asked.

"Not in the slightest," Adolf said.

The kitchen was a small room filled with large blocks of tar that could be used for chairs and a table. There was also an old black stove and a row of lockers that was used as a cupboard. There wasn't any kind of refrigerator, but the lockers were filled with canned and dehydrated food. Examining the cans: there were cans of artichoke, cans of spinach, cans of beef, cans of noodles, cans of hotdogs, cans of chocolate, cans of bread, cans of mustard, cans of fish, cans of lettuce, and cans of rainbow jelly.

"I'm the mom, I should cook," Mrs. Hitler said to Adolf, pushing him out of the kitchen. Elsie merged back into the creature's body and returned to the form of his perfect woman while he was digging through the lockers. "Sit at the table. Get acquainted with your children."

She sat Adolf down on a tar block, facing the two creatures. The girl creature was much thinner than the boy creature. Her torso was like a stick, like a praying mantis. The boy was chubby and had a reptilian mohawk on his head.

They are both hideous, Adolf thought.

"Father Eyebrows said we could have the house to ourselves for awhile if we take care of Mrs. Neat."

Adolf shrugged at her. The children were staring at him, examining his features. Opening and closing their nostrils at him and blinking slowly. Adolf stared back at them. They didn't speak to each other.

They are the most disgusting creatures I have ever seen. To think they are my offspring is utterly ridiculous. The ghost girl surely brought these creatures into my life to make me think that I have children, to trap me forever in this marriage. But I have no obligation to these children. They are not my responsibility. They are only beasts.

"I don't like them," Adolf said.

"How can you say that about your children?" said Mrs. Hitler. "Right in front of them!"

"They are abominations. They are unnatural and offensive to my genes."

"You'll learn to love them," she said.

"I will do no such thing," Adolf said.

The children didn't acknowledge their words. They continued staring at their dad with black bug eyes.

Elsie brought in plates of food. She had made hotdogs and put them on the canned bread with mustard and rainbow jelly. The meat was soggy and the bread was like moist cake but Adolf was so hungry that he ate it all within minutes. He was surprised he enjoyed the flavor of jelly mixed with tangy mustard, but the rest of it was just weird flavorless textures.

The children turned into hotdogs before eating their hotdogs. Adolf's mouth dropped open at them but Elsie just smiled in her seat as if it was the cutest thing in the world. Adolf couldn't look away as the children-sized hotdogs ate the little hotdogs.

"You have to bring me to the pet shop to get me registered today," Elsie said.

"You can go by yourself," Adolf replied. "I must go to _____ Castle."

"But I can't go alone," she said.

"Then do not go at all."

"But they will put me to sleep!"

"No, they will put that creature whose body you are possessing to sleep. You are a ghost. You can not die."

Elsie's eyes were tearing up. There was nothing that upset her more than calling her a ghost.

"But I want to stay in this body," Elsie cried. "I want to be your perfect mate."

"Fine, we will go after breakfast, but we go to the castle directly afterwards and these little creatures can not come."

"Awwww..." whined the hotdogs.

Mr. Warthog

Young Adolf dragged his leashed wife quickly through the bustling mud-caked streets of _____ City, hoping to finish with her tags as soon as possible. The citizens were puking yellow syrup into the gutters around them. Every ten feet it seemed like some creature was puking yellow gunk into something, like the whole town had just eaten the same bad food. Hitler was relieved to be wearing his yellow ceremony robe over his uniform.

"I have much to do before night falls," Adolf told his wife. "I must find a way to enter _____ Castle so that I can speak to the Golden Eel so that he can tell me where to find the place where things go so that I can find my briefcase so that I can get the picture of the imperfect man so that I can find him and exterminate him and then figure out a way to return to my normal size so that I can leave this place forever."

"But what about me?" said his wife. "You won't leave me, will you? And the kids?"

"I have a duty to my nation. I can not stay in this world."

"Can I come with you?" asked his wife.

"Most likely, no, I think not—" Adolf told his wife, but was interrupted by an angry snorting roar from behind.

He turned around to see the enormous warthog man from last night lifting his little wife in his hairy fat arms, holding her by her throat and grunting at Adolf with angry eyes.

"You killed my perfect woman," cried the warthog man. Before Adolf could react, the warthog man broke his wife's neck and tossed her corpse on the ground between them. The ghost girl emerged from the corpse, frightened and confused. When the warthog man saw Elsie, he grabbed the ghost's neck and snapped it to the side. Elsie's neck just snapped back. He picked her up over his head and tossed her at a wall, but she only passed through it without harm.

"Your woman can't die?" screamed the warthog man. "Then I will kill *you*."

The boar charged at the officer. Though Adolf believed himself to be a trained expert of hand to hand combat, his memory was still too blank to recall any fighting moves that could help him fend off the warthog man barreling towards him. He just stood there, filing through his memory, as the warthog man tackled him to the ground and raised a fist above him as big as a block of cement.

Adolf lay in a puddle of muddy yellow puke with his robe wrapped around his neck. The warthog man had stopped, frozen in his attack. He noticed something about Adolf that he hadn't noticed before. His uniform, he recognized it. Then Adolf noticed it as well. The warthog man was also wearing a Nazi uniform.

Mutant creatures stared at them in the street as they

lay there, looking at each other, wide mouths open with amazement.

"Who are you?" asked the warthog man.

"I do not know," Adolf said to the warthog man. "I arrived in this place just recently, but I have lost my memory. The people here call me Adolf Hitler because Adolf Hitler is written on my uniform."

"I, too, have lost my memory," said the warthog man, pulling them up out of the mud and wiping the puke off of their Nazi uniforms. "I also have Adolf Hitler written on my uniform. I have come to this place to find an imperfect man."

"Imperfect? In what way?" Adolf asked the warthog man.

"I am not sure," said the warthog man. "I can not remember his face, but it is imperfect. He is a disease and I am here to cure society of him."

"So am I!" Adolf said to the warthog man. "My mission is to find and destroy the last imperfect man."

"But you are so imperfect yourself," said the warthog man. "How can a creature as absurd as yourself know anything about perfection?"

"Me? Imperfect? I am the definition of perfection!"

"No, I am the definition of perfection!" said the warthog man.

"You are a beastly ogre of a man," Adolf said to the warthog man.

"You are a puny, bony, elf of a man," said the warthog man.

"How is this possible?" Adolf asked the warthog

man. "How can we be on the same mission?"

"Hmmm . . ." The warthog man scratched whiskers on his chin. "I had a partner when I started this journey. Perhaps you are my partner?"

"Yes, I too had a partner."

"What did your partner look like?" asked the warthog man.

"I do not know, but I am pretty sure he was just as perfect as myself."

"Perhaps you are my partner," said the warthog man. "But you have been hideously mutated by this strange world we are in."

"Yes, that must be the answer," Adolf said to the warthog man. "Except you are the one who has become hideously mutated, not I."

The warthog man shook his head at Adolf, but did not debate the subject further.

"We must join forces then," said the warthog man. "We can pool our resources and share information and together we will find and bring down the imperfect man for good!"

Adolf smiled and shook hands with the blubbery mutant. In the corner of his eyes, Adolf saw Elsie trying to get back inside of the dead mantimeleon, trying to possess it again, trying to make it move . . . but the flesh was dead. She could not return to the form of the perfect woman.

"Let us get a drink," said the warthog man.

Adolf nodded his head, and snapped his fingers at the ghost girl to get out of the mud and follow them.

Mr. Partner

The ghost girl whined about how the children would not accept her as their mother outside of the mantimeleon's body as they entered the pub and took a seat at the closest table to the bar. Mr. Bartender sieg heiled them and gave them two milky brown drinks before they had a chance to order anything.

"So all I remember was waking up in a giant web with very little memory of my former life," snorted the warthog man. "After a few hours, I climbed down the web and discovered there were homes and buildings all around me. People were living there, inside the giant spider's web. I was welcomed into a disgusting crippled man's home and I told him what I thought should be done with crippled people. He said to me their web community was called _____ Village. They had a textile mill on the web that harvested spider threads for clothing and curtains and such things. Eventually I was able to leave the place and was directed here to _____ City. This place is even more atrocious and absurd than _____ Village, but I figured it would be a good place to search for the imperfect man."

"Has your investigation been fertile?" Adolf asked the warthog man.

"Not quite," grunted the warthog man. "But I have questioned many people. They said there has been a stranger in the city lately who claims to be on the run from the government. I am sure it is our man. Nobody has seen him recently, though. He was sleeping on the streets and was supposed to be easy to find. I have a feeling that he has been abducted."

"Abducted?"

"People have been known to vanish from the streets at night here. There are rumors that they are being abducted by minions of the Golden Eel and brought back to the castle."

"Minions?"

"The Golden Eel is supposed to be a cruel scientist who experiments on the citizens he abducts."

"So you believe the imperfect man is somewhere in the Golden Eel's castle?"

"Yes, we must go there and have a look around. Tonight there is supposed to be a ball. I know I can get some invitations, but we will need to find dates."

"Women?"

"Yes, and there are very few women to be found in town. We can buy some at the pet shop, I guess. If only you didn't kill my perfect woman . . ."

"She was a pig!"

"She was my love! She was better than your walking corpse of a woman."

"Though much more attractive than your pig, this ghost woman is definitely an abomination. I would prefer not take her as my date to the ball."

"What if I go as your perfect woman?" asked the ghost girl. "I can possess one of the children and turn back into her."

"I guess that will work," Adolf said to the ghost girl.

"And maybe we can convince one of the other children to turn into a pig woman for your date," she said to the warthog man.

"It is not a real date," snorted the warthog man to the ghost girl, "so I will agree to this. If these children, as you call them, have the power to change form they might come in handy on our mission."

They sent Elsie back home to prepare the children for the ball that night, while Adolf and his warthog partner attempted to recollect their memories. They discovered that they both remembered the same details about their mission, yet neither of them remembered much about their past or what the imperfect man was supposed to look like.

"What I would like to know is who this Adolf Hitler person is," Adolf said to the warthog man.

"Yes, he is on my uniform as well," said the warthog man.

"Maybe he designed the uniform?"

"Or maybe he is our commanding officer?"

"Are you sure it is not a name tag?" asked the warthog man. "Are you sure you are not Adolf Hitler?"

"But you would have the same name tag then."

"Perhaps I too am Adolf Hitler."

"We both have the same first and last name?"

"I do not know. Maybe."

"It is ridiculous."

"Perhaps everyone is named Adolf Hitler where we are from."

"Preposterous!"

"Speaking of preposterous," said the warthog man, drooling from the side of his black warthog gums, "what do you think of this place we are in?"

"It should be wiped out!" Adolf said to the warthog man.

"By storm troopers!" said the warthog man.

"By blitzkrieg!"

"By missiles!"

"By neutron bomb!"

"But," began the warthog man, "how do you think this place exists? Where did it come from? Why have we never heard of it before?"

"I do not know," Adolf said to the warthog man. "It must be hidden quite well."

"I believe it was created by nature."

"By nature?"

"The world outside is totally perfect," said the warthog man. "In every way, it is utter perfection. But the universe is all about balance. Good and evil, matter and energy, perfection and imperfection... To have perfection, there must be an equal amount of imperfection."

"Blasphemy!" said young Adolf Hitler.

"This one little town of complete imperfection and total chaos exists to balance out the pure perfection that exists in the rest of the world."

"Absurd!" Adolf said to the warthog man. "Perfection can not exist with imperfection. As long as there is one smidgen of imperfection, there is no perfection. To have perfection, all flaws must be wiped out!"

"But how do you explain this town?" asked the warthog man. "If we are so perfect, then how could we let a place like this come into being?"

Adolf slammed his fist onto the table and knocked their drinks over. He didn't have anything to say, but probably would have ranted on about the absurdity of this ugly place and the ugliness of its people if he didn't notice all of the buggy mutant eyes staring at him from every corner of the room.

Mr. Conjoined

Just before twilight, after Hitler and Mr. Warthog cleaned their uniforms and obtained four counterfeit invitations to the ball from a tall smelly man with lizard arms and a beak, they met up with Elsie and the children in the middle of the dragonfly bridge. The children were now teenagers.

"Hey, dad," said the mohawked teenager.

"Hi, daddy," said the stick girl, waving.

The warthog man frowned at Adolf for bringing him into the presence of these hideous creatures.

"They grow up fast, don't they?" said the ghost girl.

Adolf frowned back at the warthog man.

"I told them I was their aunt," Elsie said. "I didn't know what else to tell them."

"These are our dates?" the Nazi warthog's eyes drooped in horror.

"They are supposed to change," Adolf told the warthog man.

Elsie snapped her white ghost fingers at the creatures.

"Just like I showed you," she told them.

Both of the creatures changed shape to look like the men's perfect mates in elegant evening gowns. Mr. Warthog's mate looked almost identical to the pig woman who died the night before.

"You are back!" cried Mr. Warthog to the pig woman.

He rushed to the pig woman and embraced her, licking her cheek. The pig woman oinked at him.

"I can't kiss you or anything," the ghost girl told Adolf as she entered the body of his perfect mate. "I'll be in your daughter's body. That would be weird."

"Perfectly acceptable," Adolf told her.

She took Adolf in her arm and complimented him on his shiny clean uniform. The four of them joined hands and practiced taking graceful ballroom steps as they marched down the dragonfly bridge towards the castle of the Golden Eel.

They walked for an hour but had yet to reach the end. The bridge was so long that for a while they could not see either end of it. They could only see the bridge and the pink and blue swirly void around them. They didn't run into anyone else on the bridge. They figured there should have been other people taking the bridge to get to the ball, but there weren't any people anywhere. They wondered if they were too late or too early.

"It is kind of lonely out here," Adolf said to the others.

The others agreed.

"Absurd and lonely," Mr. Warthog said.

"It goes on forever," said Gona.

Once _____ Castle came into view a mile farther, they all sighed with relief. The castle was large, like a mountain. It was still a few miles away, but they could tell the castle was twice as large as all of _____ City.

The architecture was chaotic and uneven. It looked like it was created at random without any predetermined design. The towers curled like goat horns, there were steel walls jagged like the face if a cliff, the balconies sagged like tongues drooping out of puffy-lipped windows. To Hitler, it was the most disgusting and imperfect work of architecture that had ever been built, and the size of the structure overwhelmed him with its enormity. It made him feel small and fragile.

The bridge ended with a column of steps that led up to the castle's only entrance. The castle seemed to be deserted as they climbed its steps. There was no light emanating from within the windows. There wasn't a sound in the air. It was dead. Adolf nearly bit his tongue when they reached the top and discovered two bodies lying on the ground near an artificial gray hedge.

Dead?

One of the dead bodies was snoring.

"I can never sleep when he's snoring," said the other dead body as they approached. "I can't sleep through the slightest noise and he can't sleep without snoring. We have to sleep in shifts."

The guards were in red uniforms with red cone hats and black eye makeup. Upon closer inspection, Adolf realized that the two guards were connected at the hip. They were conjoined twins.

"We came for the ball," Adolf said to the conjoined guard.

"The ball?" asked the conjoined guard, as if he had no idea what they were talking about.

"Yes, we have invitations," Adolf said.

The warthog man bent down and gave the reclined man the invitations.

"Invitations?" the guard was getting annoyed.

He examined the papers for two seconds and then tossed them away.

"I can't let you in," he said.

The sleeping guard snored.

"Why not?" Adolf asked. "Are we dressed inappropriately?"

"No," said the guard. "You were born inappropriately."

"What do you mean?" Adolf asked.

"Your bodies are separate!" he said. "It's offensive."

The sleeping guard snored.

"Only conjoined twins are allowed in the palace," said the awake guard. "If you want to go to the ball you have to be conjoined."

"Conjoined?" Adolf asked. "Conjoined!" Adolf raised a fist. "Siamese twins are an abomination!"

"I have orders to kill anyone who speaks ill of conjoined twins," the guard said. "The Goddesses are conjoined twins, you know."

"Goddesses?"

"The empress and her sister," said the guard. "The wives of the Golden Eel."

"Conjoined twins cannot be goddesses!" said Hitler.

"You have three options," said the reclining guard.

"You can blaspheme again and be executed on the spot, you can go back the way you came and never return, or you can go through the conjoiner and go to the ball."

The guard was strangely beginning to intimidate Adolf.

"Conjoiner?"

"It's right over there," the guard said, pointing at three booths to the left of the entrance. "It will meld two separates into conjoineds. You will not be respected as much as natural conjoineds but you will be permitted to enter _____ Castle."

"You mean I must meld my flesh to this *creature*?" Adolf asked, motioning towards the warthog man.

The guard nodded his head against the pavement. "Your dates must conjoin to each other as well."

"My body is the epitome of perfection," said Mr. Warthog. "I will never join flesh with a mutant!"

"It is the only way you can enter the castle to go to the ball. Conjoin or leave, I don't care which. Just do it quickly. I find separates disgusting and offensive."

Both Mr. Hitler and Mr. Warthog dropped their mouths at the man's preposterous opinion.

How can someone so disgusting and offensive think the same of one as perfectly beautiful as me, both Mr. Warthog and Adolf Hitler thought to themselves.

Mr. Hitlerhog

The next thing he knew, Hitler was walking through the entrance of the castle attached to the side of the sweaty warthog man. Since he was so much taller than Adolf, Mr. Warthog had to squat down while he walked so Adolf's feet could touch the ground. Their dates were also conjoined together, following closely behind.

Inside the castle, the walls were black and sweaty. Stuffed insects the size of bears decorated the hallway like displays at a museum. There were stuffed beetles, stuffed earwigs, and many stuffed dragonflies. Farther down, the insect statues were more like works of art. Parts of bugs were collaged together into grotesque new bugs. There were centipede statues with the wings of butterflies and the legs of spiders. There were cockroach statues with scorpion tails and ladybug breastplates.

The place was incredibly quiet and lonely. It looked as if nobody had walked through these halls in a decade.

"He is here, somewhere," Mr. Warthog said. "I can feel it."

"Yes," said Mr. Hitler. "This place radiates with pure imperfection. It must be the source of all the imperfection in this town. I have no doubt that the imperfect man is here, somewhere. Perhaps he is even behind everything in this town."

Their voices echoed through the dusty corridors. There weren't any other sounds besides the crackling of the withered red carpet beneath their feet.

"Should we go to the ball or should we look around?" asked Mr. Warthog.

"I assume most of the people in the castle will be at the ball," said Adolf. "If the imperfect man is a guest he will be there."

"But if he was abducted from the streets he is probably imprisoned somewhere else," said Mr. Warthog.

"We should look around," said Mr. Hitler.

The hallway ended and branched off in four different directions. Two directions were very thin diagonal hallways that they could only fit through if the warthog man sucked in his stomach and they walked sideways. They took the widest hallway to the right which was lined with smaller stuffed insects mounted on plaques like fish. There were stuffed termites, maggots, ants, ticks, fruit flies, and crab spiders.

At the end of the hallway, there was a small hatch that opened to a narrow spiral staircase descending into darkness.

"We should not travel down there," said young Adolf to the stairwell. "It could not go anywhere pleasant. We must go back and try a different direction."

"But this might lead to a dungeon that might hold the imperfect man," said Mr. Warthog.

"Perhaps," said Mr. Hitler. "But it might lead someplace unpleasant that does not hold the imperfect man. It might even lead to a sewer."

"We should look everywhere we can," said the warthog man. "It probably will not be a sewer."

Young Adolf no longer had a say in the matter after that as the warthog man started to descend the steps dragging the much smaller man with him. The women followed.

At the bottom of the black steps, they arrived in a sewer. It was lit dimly by crystal chandeliers hanging from the ceiling. The smell was thick and putrid, but more related to that of honey than that of excrement. They walked sideways along a small wooden bridge that ran alongside the river of black sludge. Young Adolf stared down at it, paranoid they might fall in.

"This is exactly where I did not want to be," said Mr. Hitler.

"Yes, but it is likely that a dungeon would be in a place such as this," said Mr. Warthog.

"Yes, but it is likely that we will be too disgusting to attend the ball after saturating ourselves in this stench."

"Yes, but we are alone down here. We can search this area freely."

"Yes, but I dislike it down here," said Mr. Hitler. "Look at the chandeliers. Why are such beautiful things in a place like this? They do not belong here."

The warthog man nearly knocked them into the sludge as he leaned forward to get a better look. "They are quite nice."

After several minutes of stepping carefully through the dimly lit sewers, they began to hear ballroom music.

There was a whispering of voices and haunting violin music echoing through the tunnels.

"The ball must be above us now," Mr. Hitler said.

"I do not think so," said Mr. Warthog. "Look up ahead."

At the end of the tunnel, Hitler discovered a large door from which the music seemed to emanate. The door was grandly decorated in gold and emerald lining. It was not the type of thing to be found in a sewer.

"This leads to the ball?" Adolf asked. "Why would they put such a grandiose entrance to a grandiose event in such a sewer?"

"Perhaps some of the guests come from the sewer," said the warthog man. Adolf shuttered.

The conjoined couples arrived in front of the door and hesitated entering. The uniformed officers attempted to rub the sewer stench from their outfits. The women wiggled their butts and oinked with excitement.

"We will blend into the crowd and search for the imperfect man," said Mr. Warthog. "If he is not there we will sneak off to more private regions of the castle."

Adolf nodded.

They opened the large doors to the ballroom. As soon as they slipped through the doors, the music and chattering stopped.

Mr. Eel

The ballroom was dead silent and mostly empty. Hitler was blinded by the whiteness of the room. There were white porcelain walls, white tiled floors, white spiderweb draperies. The only things that weren't white were the small number of guests in the room and a giant painting of a golden eel several stories high.

There were three groups of conjoined couples on the dance floor, twisting around like a windmill. Each conjoined couple of men danced with a conjoined couple of women. There wasn't any music for them to dance to, but they danced as passionately as if there were. They moved as if they were dancing to the same violin music that was playing in the sewer, but the only sound here was the tapping of their feet.

Hitler thought they were surprisingly elegant for mutants. They were yellow wasp men and green horned reptile women, but their clothing was exquisite and their movements were precisely calculated and majestic.

Hitler shook his head at himself. *No, they are only mutants. They are a mockery of true elegance.*

The room wasn't completely silent. There was an

electrical humming noise in the background and a bubbling-glugging sound. Then Hitler realized it. The giant eel painting on the other side of the ballroom was not a painting. It was an enormous aquarium containing a monstrous eel. The eel was probably only the size of a normal sea eel, but since Hitler was only the size of a tiny bug the eel seemed as enormous as a god. Hitler began to understand why the people in the underworld viewed the eel as their god.

There wasn't a way for them to blend in at this ball. The guests were so few and spread so far apart, they were instantly recognized. There were only two other couples outside of the dance floor. A couple of females and a couple of conjoined males. The two conjoined males were heading towards Adolf and the warthog man.

Trying to look inconspicuous, Hitler and the warthog man turned to their dates and pretended to be in a deep conversation that they would prefer not interrupted. Their pursuers did not catch the hint.

"Hello again," said one of the men as they arrived.

Hitler turned to see that he recognized the men. They were Mr. Eyebrows the noseless high priest and Mr. Song the pet shop owner. They had been recently conjoined and were dressed in fine jewel-studded robes like that of kings.

"It is good to see you finally made it," said Mr. Eyebrows.

He placed his arm around Adolf.

"I was expected?" asked Mr. Hitler.

"You are the guest of honor," said Mr. Eyebrows.

"I knew nothing of this," said Mr. Hitler.

"You wouldn't have," said Mr. Eyebrows. "You were just now chosen as the guest of honor by the Goddess."

Mr. Eyebrows pointed at one of the women across the dance floor by the eel tank. He then noticed that the two women over there were not conjoined.

"I thought the Goddess was conjoined?" Adolf said.

"Yeah," said the warthog man. "They said everyone has to be conjoined to match her."

"Oh, yes," said Mr. Eyebrows. "They used to be conjoined but were separated a few days ago. They are much happier now that they are separated."

"But I thought being separated was offensive?" Adolf asked.

"Oh, it is," said Mr. Song. "It most definitely is."

Hitler wondered why the empress would be held in such high regard yet all other women were considered mere pets. Even Mr. Song and Mr. Eyebrows, who previously seemed to abhor women, were deeply respectful of her. *Are the gender roles different in _____ Castle than they are in _____ City? It does not make any sense.*

"Nevermind about that," said Mr. Eyebrows. "Come, as the guest of honor you must meet the Golden Eel and his wife."

The conjoined Mr. Eyebrowsong took the conjoined Mr. Hitlerhog towards the large eel aquarium. Young Adolf noticed that the eel was not actually golden in color. It was wearing scaled plates of gold. The closer Hitler got to the eel, the more common-looking the eel became. It didn't look like a brilliant god-like being to him at all. It was just like an ordinary eel, only hundreds of times the size. It's eyes gazed off into space.

"Does it speak?" asked young Adolf.

"Never address him as *it*," said Mr. Song.

"Does he speak?" asked young Adolf.

"Not to us," said Mr. Eyebrows. "Only the Goddess can speak to the great Golden Eel."

"Has anyone ever seen the eel do anything aside from swim in the tank of water?" asked young Adolf.

"Yes, the Goddess tells of many great things he has done in the past. The Golden Eel is brilliant and is responsible for all the marvels of our world."

"But have you or has anyone you know, besides the Goddess, ever seen the Golden Eel do anything besides swim in the aquarium?" asked young Adolf.

Mr. Eyebrows looked at Mr. Song. Mr. Song shrugged.

"No," said Mr. Eyebrows. "We are not permitted to associate with the Golden Eel. Only the Goddess knows of his secret activities."

"This is not unusual to you?" asked young Adolf.

"As they say, the Golden Eel works in mysterious ways," said Mr. Eyebrows.

Mrs. Eel

The Goddess and her sister were standing beneath the Golden Eel's aquarium, staring up at the monstrous creature. Both of the women's heads were completely encased in bandages. One was wearing a green plaid skirt and the other was wearing a red plaid skirt. Aside from the skirts, the women were nude, exposing their naked breasts to the giant eel and rubbing their bodies with oil.

Because their faces were bandaged up like mummies with dark red spots on the side where the blood soaked through, Adolf assumed the women used to be conjoined by the sides of their heads. Aside from the mummy faces, the women looked human to Adolf. Not only human, but they almost seemed attractive to him. Their bodies were perfectly acceptable. Their breasts almost three times the size of his perfect woman's.

Adolf changed his mind as Mr. Eyebrows took them closer to the women. They were missing limbs. The one in the red skirt was missing a hand and half of a foot. The one in green was missing an arm all the way up to the shoulder. And between their legs, sprouting out from under their skirts, there were dozens of thin squirming tentacles. Not the tentacles of a squid, but those of a jellyfish or a sea anemone. They were growing out of their crotches like long horrific pubic hair.

These women are not human, they are creatures like the rest.

Adolf felt nausea rising in his throat as he realized that the oil they were rubbing on their bodies was actually a clear jelly that they were milking out of their pubic tentacles. The odor of the jelly was similar to that of black olives.

"Your Highness," Mr. Eyebrows said to the women. "There are some people who would like to meet you."

The two women turned to face Adolf and his company. Even though their eyes were beneath the bandages, it was as if they could still see through them.

"Ah yes, Mr. Adolf Hitler," said a whispery female voice.

The voice seemed to come from neither of the women but from somewhere beyond them. With their mouths under the bandages, Adolf could not tell if either one of them had spoken.

"I am not really Adolf Hitler," said young Adolf Hitler. "I do not know what my name is. My memory has disappeared. All I know is that I am on a quest."

The two women stared at Adolf for a while. They shifted their greasy bellies from side to side and breathed deeply through the gauze.

"I am on a quest to find an imperfect man. I believe he is somewhere in this castle. Perhaps you might be of some assistance?"

The two women continued staring. Their harsh

breathes became louder, wheezing through the fabric at him. The one in the red skirt caressed her greasy thigh.

"It is a matter of national security," said young Adolf.

The women wheezed and shifted.

"Imperfect?" said a rough whispery female voice. "In..." It paused to take a deep breath. "...what way?"

"I, uh—" Adolf rubbed sweat from his brow. He didn't know which woman was speaking, so his eyes focused on the space between them as he spoke. "I am not sure."

The women cocked their bandaged heads at him. He looked at the warthog man for answers, but his conjoined brother was lost in thought.

"I can not remember his face, but it is imperfect," Adolf said, composing himself. "He is a disease and I am here—"

The raspy voice cut him off. "Are you against imperfection?"

Adolf hesitated. "Y-yes. I believe perfection is all that is good and imperfection is all that is evil."

"Yes," said the voice, hissing like a snake.

Then Adolf realized that it was the red-skirted woman speaking to him. Her head moved when the voice last spoke.

Or did it? Yes, it must have. The one in red must be the Goddess, the wife of the Golden Eel.

"I agree," said Mrs. Eel. "Imperfection must be wiped out. Only the perfect should be allowed to live."

"Yes," said Mr. Hitler. "My quest is to eliminate the last imperfect man so that I can bring perfection to the human gene pool."

"I, too, am on a quest, Mr. Hitler," whispered Mrs. Eel. "My quest is in a similar vein."

The red-skirted woman stepped closer to Adolf and the warthog man, filling their nostrils with her strong black olive scent.

"Come with me," she said. "I must show you my progress."

The half-naked women pushed them aside like they were opening a door and stepped slowly across the dance floor towards a hole in the center of the room. They walked sluggishly with a rolling bounce that made them look as if they were walking under water.

"You must have impressed her," said Mr. Eyebrows. "I've never heard of her showing anyone her work before."

"If she works in *perfection*," said Mr. Hitler, "then it is understandable. I am probably the most *perfect* example of a human she has ever seen."

"Good luck," said Mr. Song.

Hitler and the warthog man waved them goodbye and followed after the Goddess and her sister. Their conjoined dates stayed behind, frowning at the ground as if they had just been dumped for the large-breasted mummy-faced women.

In the center of the ballroom, there was a black circle. Mr. Hitlerhog dodged the conjoined dancers and arrived in the center where the two half-naked women waited for them. The silent dancers windmilled around them.

"Ready?" asked Mrs. Eel in her whispery voice.

Adolf nodded.

Then the black circle began to descend like an elevator.

Mr. Master Race

They descended down into a dungeon world miles below the ballroom floor. It was dark and a thick fog was pouring against them. They were descending into a smoke-filled industrial wasteland. The sound of churning, grinding machines could be heard far below.

The elevator didn't have any railing, so Adolf squeezed in close to the women so that his chances of falling off would decrease. He was close enough to Mrs. Eel that he could feel the warmth coming off of her olive-oiled body. He could feel her jellyfish tentacles coiling around his legs. She said nothing, though, just staring at him without eyes and wheezing through her bandages.

The closer they got to the bottom, the louder the machines became. Adolf heard crushing, grinding, buzzing, screeching, screaming. It was as if something was alive down there. Like thousands of mechanical dinosaurs were ripping each other apart. As they descended, the volume of the machines tore at their ears. Hitler cowered towards the center of the platform.

Once the view of the machines burst into Adolf's eyesight, he jumped forward as if he was under attack.

There were thousands of enormous machine-creatures screaming and thrashing about. Adolf pressed himself against Mrs. Eel, caring not that she was bare-chested, nor that she was a Goddess. They weren't mechanical dinosaurs, but they looked very much like mechanical dinosaur-sized beetles and millipedes. As they ripped into each other, Adolf figured they must have had some kind of purpose. Perhaps they were generators or construction equipment. The technology was beyond Adolf's understanding.

The platform continued descending below the industrial level and into a lower complex. They passed a level filled with orange-suited factory workers, then passed a refrigerated level filled with dozens of giant dead fish, then a level of empty black prison cells.

Adolf realized he was still leaning against Mrs. Eel's naked body. He pulled himself away from her to discover his uniform was now saturated in her olive-oil sweat. He looked at her. She was still staring at him.

If these primitive people think of her as a Goddess, even though it is absurd that such a creature would be considered a goddess, she could have me executed for touching her in such a way.

"Sorry," young Adolf said to the Goddess. "Please forgive me." It was hard for him to sound sincere.

"For what?" asked Mrs. Eel.

They passed a level of small makeshift barracks with six red checkered beds cluttered together. A cow-headed man was sitting on one of them, staring at Adolf while licking a black leather shoe.

"For touching you in such a way," said young Adolf. "I know it is inappropriate."

"Men are silly creatures," whispered Mrs. Eel. "They are like children."

"You talk as if men are less than women?" asked young Adolf.

"Of course they are," said Mrs. Eel. "Women are far superior to men in every way."

"Then why do men think of women as mere pets here?" asked young Adolf. "Why are women considered third class citizens?"

"Men are easy to control," said Mrs. Eel. "It is the women I worry about."

They passed a deserted child's playground level.

"I keep their social status equal to animals," continued Mrs. Eel, "to keep them from using their brains. I haven't had any problems since."

They passed another level that contained an enormous miniature city filled with micro-sized people that were one-hundredth the size of Adolf even in his shrunken state. It was a bustling metropolis, filled with millions of micro-sized beings. As they descended, Mrs. Eel rubbed her index finger along the side of one of the miniature high-rise buildings. Once her finger reached street level she pressed it against the sidewalk, crushing a miniature business man on his way to work. She rubbed his bloody remains against the side of her chest and hip.

They finally arrived in a sterile laboratory environment and the platform came to a stop.

"Here," Mrs. Eel rasp-whispered, stepping off of the platform.

The others followed her down a hallway to a large red door. She opened a panel next to the door and placed her hand within a green soup. It was some kind of identity scan. The door beeped and opened. The Goddess rubbed the goopy hand all over the side of her chest and hip until the slime was absorbed into her skin.

They entered what looked like an enormous morgue to Adolf. There were dozens of rows of tables containing bodies. Several hundred bodies. Dead mutant creatures.

"I believe you will be impressed with my work so far," said Mrs. Eel. "I want to create a race of utter beauty and perfection. I want to create a master race."

She took them down an aisle of tables.

"I have been kidnapping people from the streets to use in my research," she continued. "I take the best genes from people and implant them into my specimens."

Adolf sneered in disgust at the creatures around him. They were horrible mutants, even worse than the creatures of _____ City.

"That is why we came," said Mr. Warthog. "We believe the man we are searching for was taken from the streets and brought here. Have you taken him?"

"Perhaps," said Mrs. Eel. "Many people are used in my research."

Adolf saw one of the bodies move on a table he passed. He wondered if the bodies were all still alive.

"Would he be dead if he was taken here?" asked Mr. Warthog.

"Perhaps," said Mrs. Eel. "Many people die in my research."

She took them to the far end of the room to another door. She turned to face them. Her sister leaned her back against the wall.

"I have chosen you to be the first to meet my new creation," said Mrs. Eel. "I have never before met anyone, besides my sister, who cared of perfection. Our entire lives we were told that perfection is impossible. Everything is imperfect."

"Nonsense," said Mr. Warthog.

"Complete nonsense," said Mr. Hitler. "Perfection is the only thing one must strive for."

"I agree," said Mrs. Eel. "While I am not fond of you as men, I am fond of your ideals. Therefore, I will honor you with a glimpse at perfection."

She opened the door and led them inside.

"Here it is," said Mrs. Eel. "The most perfect being you will ever see."

As Adolf entered, he noticed the large caged in habitat. Inside there was a large creature. Its skin was gray and armored. It had wings like a bat's, eyes like an eagle's, teeth like a shark's, and claws of metal. It was part insect, part reptile, part demon. It was the most hideous monstrosity Adolf had ever seen.

"What do you think?" asked Mrs. Eel.

Both Adolf and the warthog man were paralyzed with disgust. The creature was oozing fluids. It produced an odor that was similar to rancid chicken.

"Well?" asked Mrs. Eel. "Isn't he magnificent?"

The creature licked its eyeballs with a long frog tongue.

"It is . . ." Adolf began. "It is the most horrible, imperfect creature I have ever seen."

Adolf said the wrong thing. Even though the Goddess' face was completely covered, he could still see the rage building up beneath the bandages.

"Imperfect?" asked Mrs. Eel. "What do you know of perfection, you pathetic man?"

"What do I know of perfection?" said young Adolf, raising his voice to her. "I am the living embodiment of perfection! There have never been genes more refined than mine and that of my people!"

"You! Perfect?" whisper-screamed Mrs. Eel. "You think you are superior to my creation?"

"Yes, I am obviously far superior," said Mr. Hitler.

"Can you hear a conversation seventy miles away?" asked Mrs. Eel.

Young Adolf raised his eyebrows in confusion.

"... What?"

"Are your ears powerful enough to clearly hear things over seventy miles away?" Then she pointed at her beast. "Because he can. Can you fly or breathe underwater?"

"No," said Adolf.

"Well, he can," she said. "He also has claws that can cut through steel. He can read a novel from hundreds of feet away, even in the dark. He can run up to ninety miles-per-hour. He is stronger than ten bears. His skin is nearly impenetrable. He hardly needs to eat or sleep. He is immune to all known diseases and can live for over five hundred years. He is far superior."

"Perhaps he is physically superior," said young Adolf. "But so is a machine. There are surely vehicles that can fly faster than this creature. There are surely lasers that can cut steel with greater ease. But these are just tools. Your creation is also just a tool. I will admit that you have created a powerful tool, but it is still only a tool. It does not have a superior mind."

Mrs. Eel snickered. "His mind is his most powerful feature. His memory is so efficient that he never has and never will forget anything he has ever seen. He has perfect math and analysis skills. He can learn any language almost instantly. He can think and strategize quicker than any other living creature ever born. His brain is a super brain. It is my greatest achievement."

"But surely it is like a computer," said Adolf. "Computers are still just tools. Its brain is only a super computer made of flesh. It could never have the creative and artistic talent that I process."

"He does have artistic talent," said Mrs. Eel, "only it is far more evolved than anything you could ever comprehend. Every attempt at art has resulted in masterpiece after masterpiece. What takes the greatest artists, writers, and musicians a lifetime to achieve takes him half of an afternoon."

"But where is its passion and emotional depth?" said young Adolf. "It does not have the ability to feel as I do. It does not have the soul. Your creature might be physically and mentally superior, but I have the superior soul. That is what really matters."

"A superior soul?" asked Mrs. Eel. "What does that even mean? How can one measure the worth of a soul?"

"If you do not know then obviously your creation is deficient in soul," said young Adolf.

"There's no proof that souls are even real," said Mrs. Eel.

"Perhaps you are just too inferior to understand

the complexities of the human soul," said young Adolf. "No, your creature is nothing compared to me. Just look at him. He is disgusting. My kind, we are pure beauty. We are the definition of perfection."

"No, you're not!" cried Mrs. Eel. "You are inferior. You are ugly. My creation is the most beautiful being in existence. His beauty is his greatest quality. It is his most perfect quality."

"He is pitiful and ugly," said young Adolf. "You only believe him to have perfect beauty, because your brain is flawed. You do not understand true perfection as I do."

The Goddess slapped Adolf across his face.

He crossed the line with that last remark. The warthog man covered Hitler's mouth so that he could not speak anymore.

"Very well," said Mrs. Eel. "We will see how your superior soul holds up against my superior being."

Mr. Imperfect

The next thing Adolf knew, he was in a great arena, still attached to the warthog man who was shaking and drooling sweat all over his uniform.

There were thousands of people in the stadium seated all around him. Closest to the ground were the citizens of _____ City. He saw Elsie in the crowd with his mutant children, no longer conjoined, waving nervously at him. He saw Mr. Eyebrows and Mr. Song. He saw the conjoined guards that he met outside of _____ Castle. He even saw Mrs. Neat, sitting quietly in her racecar shell on Mr. Eyebrows' lap.

Up higher in the stands, there was Mr. Handlebar Mustache and the other cockroach people from the above world. High above them, Adolf saw a dozen giants gathered around the coliseum. There was Mr. Wheel, hovering over the stadium with a crooked grin on his face. And there was the bartender, passing out beers to the other giants above.

Inside the arena, Adolf saw Mrs. Eel's creature standing before him. It waited patiently, wagging a black spiked tail. Beyond the creature, their god, the Golden

Eel, was swimming in a giant tank of water. The Goddess and her sister were by his side.

"We have no chance," said Mr. Warthog. "It will tear us to pieces."

"I will not allow myself to be killed by such an imperfect creature," said Mr. Hitler.

"You are an imperfect creature yourself," said Mr. Warthog.

"I am the definition of perfection," said Mr. Hitler.

"You really are not," said Mr. Warthog.

Adolf raised his fist to the warthog man. He didn't realize that Mrs. Eel had given the signal for the battle to begin. It was over before Adolf knew what had happened.

"What the hell do you know?" Adolf screamed at the warthog man as his torso was ripped in half.

Adolf watched as the warthog man ran away with part of his torso, including one of his arms and one of his legs, still attached. His blood sprayed out all over the coliseum floor. He didn't realize that the mutant creature had cut him practically in half until he had fallen to the ground.

Bleeding to death, Adolf watched as the creature chased down the warthog man and sliced off his head. It shredded his obese body, tearing chunks of meat out of him and guzzling down his entrails.

"Hideous," Adolf muttered, watching the beast. "Imperfect and hideous."

Elsie jumped down from the stadium balcony and ran across the arena to him. She picked up his halved body and held it in her arms.

"No, you can't leave me," she cried. "I was just

starting to feel human again."

Adolf coughed up some blood at her.

"I can not die," he said. "I have to get the other half of my torso back from the warthog man, so that I can sew myself back together, so that I can kill that hideous creature, so that I can prove to the empress that I am a perfect being, so that she will help me find the imperfect man, so that I can eliminate him and return home a hero to the nation, so that I can . . ."

Adolf's eyes rolled into the back of his head and his body went limp.

"No," Elsie cried. "Stay with me. You can't go. You must stay."

Adolf felt his soul slip out of his body. His soul was sinking, floating down below the surface of the earth.

Elsie's ghost hand reached through his body and caught his soul under the ground.

"You can't go," she said. "You must stay with me. I don't want to be alone again."

His soul sunk deeper underground. She attempted to pull him out, but her fingers were slipping.

"I don't care if you're just a ghost," she cried. "We can just pretend to be alive. We can pretend forever."

"You are an atrocity," said young Adolf's soul beneath the ground. "You should not even exist."

He slipped out of her hands and drifted deep into the earth. She was crying too loudly to hear his words.

For what seemed like days, Adolf's soul floated downward through rock and mineral. He felt dazed and at peace. He had died and slipped into this eternal slumber. But his quest was not over yet.

As soon as he regained consciousness, Adolf felt himself falling out of rock and into hollow space. He floated through air. The world around him was pink and white. He rolled over and looked down. Below him was a cartoon world filled with dancing dinnerplates and singing candlesticks. There were candy houses and fuzzy bright orange grass fields.

When he landed on the ground, he felt no pain. He felt nothing at all. His eyes blinked in and out of consciousness. He was still in a dazed post-life mindset. Everything around him was a strange illusion.

Three of the citizens of this brightly-colored cartoon world came up to Adolf to see if he was okay. There was a blue female gravy boat walking on stubby little legs, a brown suitcase with a thin mustache, and an acoustic guitar with long shaggy hair.

"Are you okay, mister?" asked the acoustic guitar. "You sure did fall a long way."

Hitler decided to humor his hallucinations. He had nothing better to do.

"I feel fine," Adolf said. "No harm done."

"That's great," said the gravy boat. "It would have been awful if you would have hurt yourself."

"I feel fine," Adolf said, his head swaying from side to side. "Really."

"What are doing down here, Max?" asked the suitcase.

"I am on a quest," Adolf said. "Wait . . . what did you just call me?"

"Max," said the suitcase. "That's your name isn't it?"

"No," he said. "It is Adol— I do not know my name."

"Lost your memory, huh?" asked the acoustic guitar.

"Yeah," said Adolf.

"You said you were on a quest?" asked the gravy boat. "Tell us about your quest. Maybe that will jog your memory."

"I am on a quest to find the last imperfect man," said Adolf. "Have you seen him?"

"Imperfect?" asked the suitcase. "In what way?"

"I am not sure," said Adolf. "I can not remember his face, but it is imperfect. He is a disease and I am here to cure society of him."

"Sounds terrible," said the acoustic guitar.

"I have a picture of him in my briefcase," said Adolf. "If only I could find my briefcase I would know the man I seek."

"Am I your briefcase?" asked the suitcase.

"What?" asked Adolf.

Adolf's vision began to clear. His hallucination was wearing off and reality was pouring in. However, the cartoon characters were not part of the hallucination, they were real. Only they no longer looked like cartoons. They looked like a real guitar, gravy boat, and briefcase.

Briefcase?

Adolf realized that the brown suitcase was not a suitcase. It was a briefcase. He didn't remember exactly what his briefcase looked like, but for some reason it clicked in his head that this living creature really was his briefcase.

"Let me see," Adolf said.

He picked up the briefcase and unlocked the latches.

"Wait!" cried the briefcase. "Don't open me up!"

When Adolf opened it, the briefcase screamed in pain as all of his guts spilled out onto the ground.

"You killed him!" cried the acoustic guitar.

"Run away!" cried the gravy boat.

Then they ran away.

The briefcase was limp and lifeless. Adolf picked through his guts, which were really just papers and notebooks.

This is it, he thought. *This is my briefcase. I have finally found it.*

He found the file of the man he was looking for. The imperfect man. He picked his photo out of the pile and took a good look at it.

"Yes, he is the one," Adolf said.

The image was of a man who looked nearly identical to Hitler. He had the same hair. The same skin color. The same eye color. The same height. Very similar facial features. There was only one difference between them. The earlobes of the man in the photo were joined to his head, rather than hanging.

"Quite the horrific genetic flaw," Adolf said.

He put the papers back into his briefcase and stood up.

"I will not give up now," Adolf said. "This disease to the human gene pool must be stopped."

He walked through this new world of animated objects and pink furry landscapes. He wiped his soul clean, realizing that he was no long cut in half. He was wearing his uniform again, now perfectly straightened and spotless.

"I now must find a way out of this place," said young Adolf Hitler, "so that I can go back to _____ City, so that I can possess one of my mutant children as the ghost girl had, so that I can become human again, so that I can work on recovering more of my memory, so that I can track down the imperfect man, so that I can exterminate him, so that I go back to _____ Castle, so that I can figure out a way to return to my normal size, so that I can return to my perfect world, so that I can become a hero to the nation, so that I can live a life of peace and harmony and *perfection* for all of eternity."

Forever.

"The greater the emphasis on perfection, the further it recedes."

- Haridas Chaudhuri

the AVANT PUNK BOOK CLUB

SUBSCRIBE NOW!

Tired of trying to track down books by Carlton Mellick III? Sick of the long wait from amazon.com or bugging Barnes and Noble to actually put the rotten things on their shelves? Then you should subscribe to **The Avant Punk Book Club**! For $55, you will get the next six Carlton Mellick III books released through Avant Punk sent directly to your home *one month before their release dates!* No more waiting, no more hassle. Just razor wire butt plugs all year round!

Please fill out the form and mail it to the address below with a check or money order for $55 made out to Rose O'Keefe. You can also pay online via paypal.com to publisher@eraserheadpress.com, just put "Avant Punk Book Club" in the subject line. NOTE: these books will be released on an irregular basis, but CM3 is shooting for a bi-monthly writing schedule. There might also be the occasional Mellick-approved guest Bizarro author book released through the Avant Punk Book Club, but no more than one or two of the six.

Rose O'Keefe / Eraserhead Press
205 NE Bryant
Portland, OR 97211

Name_____
Address_____
City_____State____Zip_____

ABOUT THE AUTHOR

Carlton Mellick III is one of the leading authors in the new *Bizarro* genre uprising. In only a few short years, his surreal counterculture novels have drawn an international cult following despite the fact that they have been shunned by most libraries and corporate bookstores. He sings for the band "Popes That Are Porn Stars" in Portland, OR.

Visit him online at **www.carltonmellick.com**

Bizarro books

CATALOGUE – SPRING 2008

Bizarro Books publishes under the following imprints:

www.rawdogscreamingpress.com

www.eraserheadpress.com

www.afterbirthbooks.com

www.swallowdownpress.com

For all your Bizarro needs visit:

WWW.BIZARROCENTRAL.COM

Introduce yourselves to the bizarro genre and all of its authors with the *Bizarro Starter Kit* series. Each volume features short novels and short stories by ten of the leading bizarro authors, designed to give you a perfect sampling of the genre for only $5 plus shipping.

BB-0X1
"The Bizarro Starter Kit"
(Orange)

Featuring D. Harlan Wilson, Carlton Mellick III, Jeremy Robert Johnson, Kevin L Donihe, Gina Ranalli, Andre Duza, Vincent W. Sakowski, Steve Beard, John Edward Lawson, and Bruce Taylor.

236 pages $5

BB-0X2
"The Bizarro Starter Kit"
(Blue)

Featuring Ray Fracalossy, Jeremy C. Shipp, Jordan Krall, Mykle Hansen, Andersen Prunty, Eckhard Gerdes, Bradley Sands, Steve Aylett, Christian TeBordo, and Tony Rauch.

244 pages $5

BB-001 "The Kafka Effekt" D. Harlan Wilson - A collection of forty-four irreal short stories loosely written in the vein of Franz Kafka, with more than a pinch of William S. Burroughs sprinkled on top. **211 pages $14**

BB-002 "Satan Burger" Carlton Mellick III - The cult novel that put Carlton Mellick III on the map ... Six punks get jobs at a fast food restaurant owned by the devil in a city violently overpopulated by surreal alien cultures. **236 pages $14**

BB-003 "Some Things Are Better Left Unplugged" Vincent Sakwoski - Join The Man and his Nemesis, the obese tabby, for a nightmare roller coaster ride into this postmodern fantasy. **152 pages $10**

BB-004 "Shall We Gather At the Garden?" Kevin L Donihe - Donihe's Debut novel. Midgets take over the world, The Church of Lionel Richie vs. The Church of the Byrds, plant porn and more! **244 pages $14**

BB-005 "Razor Wire Pubic Hair" Carlton Mellick III - A genderless humandildo is purchased by a razor dominatrix and brought into her nightmarish world of bizarre sex and mutilation. **176 pages $11**

BB-006 "Stranger on the Loose" D. Harlan Wilson - The fiction of Wilson's 2nd collection is planted in the soil of normalcy, but what grows out of that soil is a dark, witty, otherworldly jungle... **228 pages $14**

BB-007 "The Baby Jesus Butt Plug" Carlton Mellick III - Using clones of the Baby Jesus for anal sex will be the hip sex fetish of the future. **92 pages $10**

BB-008 "Fishyfleshed" Carlton Mellick III - The world of the past is an illogical flatland lacking in dimension and color, a sick-scape of crispy squid people wandering the desert for no apparent reason. **260 pages $14**

BB-009 **"Dead Bitch Army"** Andre Duza - Step into a world filled with racist teenagers, cannibals, 100 warped Uncle Sams, automobiles with razor-sharp teeth, living graffiti, and a pissed-off zombie bitch out for revenge. 344 pages $16

BB-010 **"The Menstruating Mall"** Carlton Mellick III *"The Breakfast Club* meets *Chopping Mall* as directed by David Lynch." - Brian Keene 212 pages $12

BB-011 **"Angel Dust Apocalypse"** Jeremy Robert Johnson - Meth-heads, man-made monsters, and murderous Neo-Nazis. "Seriously amazing short stories..." - Chuck Palahniuk, author of *Fight Club* 184 pages $11

BB-012 **"Ocean of Lard"** Kevin L Donihe / Carlton Mellick III - A parody of those old Choose Your Own Adventure kid's books about some very odd pirates sailing on a sea made of animal fat. 176 pages $12

BB-013 **"Last Burn in Hell"** John Edward Lawson - From his lurid angst-affair with a lesbian music diva to his ascendance as unlikely pop icon the one constant for Kenrick Brimley, official state prison gigolo, is he's got no clue what he's doing. 172 pages $14

BB-014 **"Tangerinephant"** Kevin Dole 2 - TV-obsessed aliens have abducted Michael Tangerinephant in this bizarro combination of science fiction, satire, and surrealism. 164 pages $11

BB-015 **"Foop!"** Chris Genoa - Strange happenings are going on at Dactyl, Inc, the world's first and only time travel tourism company.
"A surreal pie in the face!" - Christopher Moore 300 pages $14

BB-016 **"Spider Pie"** Alyssa Sturgill - A one-way trip down a rabbit hole inhabited by sexual deviants and friendly monsters, fairytale beginnings and hideous endings. 104 pages $11

BB-017 **"The Unauthorized Woman"** Efrem Emerson - Enter the world of the inner freak, a landscape populated by the pre-dead and morticioners, by cockroaches and 300-lb robots. **104 pages $11**

BB-018   **"Fugue XXIX"** Forrest Aguirre - Tales from the fringe of speculative literary fiction where innovative minds dream up the future's uncharted territories while mining forgotten treasures of the past. **220 pages $16**

BB-019   **"Pocket Full of Loose Razorblades"** John Edward Lawson - A collection of dark bizarro stories. From a giant rectum to a foot-fungus factory to a girl with a biforked tongue. **190 pages $13**

BB-020 **"Punk Land"**   Carlton Mellick III - In the punk version of Heaven, the anarchist utopia is threatened by corporate fascism and only Goblin, Mortician's sperm, and a blue-mohawked female assassin named Shark Girl can stop them. **284 pages $15**

BB-021 **"Pseudo-City"** D. Harlan Wilson - Pseudo-City exposes what waits in the bathroom stall, under the manhole cover and in the corporate boardroom, all in a way that can only be described as mind-bogglingly irreal. **220 pages $16**

BB-022   **"Kafka's Uncle and Other Strange Tales"** Bruce Taylor - Anslenot and his giant tarantula (tormentor? fri-end?) wander a desecrated world in this novel and collection of stories from Mr. Magic Realism Himself. **348 pages $17**

BB-023 **"Sex and Death In Television Town"** Carlton Mellick III - In the old west, a gang of hermaphrodite gunslingers take refuge from a demon plague in Telos: a town where its citizens have televisions instead of heads. **184 pages $12**

BB-024   **"It Came From Below The Belt"** Bradley Sands - What can Grover Goldstein do when his severed, sentient penis forces him to return to high school and help it win the presidential election? **204 pages $13**

BB-025 "Sick: An Anthology of Illness" John Lawson, editor - These Sick stories are horrendous and hilarious dissections of creative minds on the scalpel's edge. **296 pages $16**

BB-026 "Tempting Disaster" John Lawson, editor - A shocking and alluring anthology from the fringe that examines our culture's obsession with taboos. **260 pages $16**

BB-027 "Siren Promised" Jeremy Robert Johnson - Nominated for the Bram Stoker Award. A potent mix of bad drugs, bad dreams, brutal bad guys, and surreal/incredible art by Alan M. Clark. **190 pages $13**

BB-028 "Chemical Gardens" Gina Ranalli - Ro and punk band *Green is the Enemy* find Kreepkins, a surfer-dude warlock, a vengeful demon, and a Metal Priestess in their way as they try to escape an underground nightmare. **188 pages $13**

BB-029 "Jesus Freaks" Andre Duza For God so loved the world that he gave his only two begotten sons... and a few million zombies. **400 pages $16**

BB-030 "Grape City" Kevin L. Donihe - More Donihe-style comedic bizarro about a demon named Charles who is forced to work a minimum wage job on Earth after Hell goes out of business. **108 pages $10**

BB-031 "Sea of the Patchwork Cats" Carlton Mellick III - A quiet dreamlike tale set in the ashes of the human race. For Mellick enthusiasts who also adore *The Twilight Zone*. **112 pages $10**

BB-032 "Extinction Journals" Jeremy Robert Johnson - An uncanny voyage across a newly nuclear America where one man must confront the problems associated with loneliness, insane dieties, radiation, love, and an ever-evolving cockroach suit with a mind of its own. **104 pages $10**

BB-033 "Meat Puppet Cabaret" Steve Beard At last! The secret connection between Jack the Ripper and Princess Diana's death revealed!   **240 pages $16 / $30**

BB-034 "The Greatest Fucking Moment in Sports" Kevin L. Donihe - In the tradition of the surreal anti-sitcom *Get A Life* comes a tale of triumph and agape love from the master of comedic bizarro.   **108 pages $10**

BB-035 "The Troublesome Amputee" John Edward Lawson - Disturbing verse from a man who truly believes nothing is sacred and intends to prove it. **104 pages $9**

BB-036 "Deity" Vic Mudd   God (who doesn't like to be called "God") comes down to a typical, suburban, Ohio family for a little vacation—but it doesn't turn out to be as relaxing as He had hoped it would be...   **168 pages $12**

BB-037 "The Haunted Vagina" Carlton Mellick III - It's difficult to love a woman whose vagina is a gateway to the world of the dead.   **132 pages $10**

BB-038 "Tales from the Vinegar Wasteland" Ray Fracalossy - Witness: a man is slowly losing his face, a neighbor who periodically screams out for no apparent reason, and a house with a room that doesn't actually exist.   **240 pages $14**

BB-039 "Suicide Girls in the Afterlife" Gina Ranalli - After Pogue commits suicide, she unexpectedly finds herself an unwilling "guest" at a hotel in the Afterlife, where she meets a group of bizarre characters, including a goth Satan, a hippie Jesus, and an alien-human hybrid.   **100 pages $9**

BB-040 "And Your Point Is?" Steve Aylett - In this follow-up to LINT multiple authors provide critical commentary and essays about Jeff Lint's mind-bending literature. **104 pages $11**

BB-041 **"Not Quite One of the Boys"** Vincent Sakowski -While drug-dealer Maxi drinks with Dante in purgatory, God and Satan play a little tri-level chess and do a little bargaining over his business partner, Vinnie, who is still left on earth. **220 pages $14**

BB-042 **"Teeth and Tongue Landscape"** Carlton Mellick III - On a planet made out of meat, a socially-obsessive monophobic man tries to find his place amongst the strange creatures and communities that he comes across. **110 pages $10**

BB-043 **"War Slut"** Carlton Mellick III - Part "1984," part "Waiting for Godot," and part action horror video game adaptation of John Carpenter's "The Thing." **116 pages $10**

BB-044 **"All Encompassing Trip"** Nicole Del Sesto -In a world where coffee is no longer available, the only television shows are reality TV re-runs, and the animals are talking back, Nikki, Amber and a singing Coyote in a do-rag are out to restore the light **308 pages $15**

BB-045 **"Dr. Identity"** D. Harlan Wilson - Follow the Dystopian Duo on a killing spree of epic proportions through the irreal postcapitalist city of Bliptown where time ticks sideways, artificial Bug-Eyed Monsters punish citizens for consumer-capitalist lethargy, and ultraviolence is as essential as a daily multivitamin. **208 pages $15**

BB-046 **"The Million-Year Centipede"** Eckhard Gerdes -Wakelin, frontman for 'The Hinge,' wrote a poem so prophetic that to ignore it dooms a person to drown in blood. **130 pages $12**

BB-047 **"Sausagey Santa"** Carlton Mellick III - A bizarro Christmas tale featuring Santa as a piratey mutant with a body made of sausages. **124 pages $10**

BB-048 **"Misadventures in a Thumbnail Universe"** Vincent Sakowski - Dive deep into the surreal and satirical realms of neo-classical Blender Fiction, filled with television shoes and flesh-filled skies. **120 pages $10**

BB-049 "Vacation" Jeremy C. Shipp - Blueblood Bernard Johnson left his boring life behind to go on The Vacation, a year-long corporate sponsored odyssey. But instead of seeing the world, Bernard is captured by terrorists, becomes a key figure in secret drug wars, and, worse, doesn't once miss his secure American Dream. **160 pages $14**

BB-050 "Discouraging at Best" John Edward Lawson - A collection where the absurdity of the mundane expands exponentially creating a tidal wave that sweeps reason away. For those who enjoy satire, bizarro, or a good old-fashioned slap to the senses. **208 pages $15**

BB-051 "13 Thorns" Gina Ranalli - Thirteen tales of twisted, bizarro horror. **240 pages $13**

BB-052 "Better Ways of Being Dead" Christian TeBordo - In this class, the students have to keep one palm down on the table at all times, and listen to lectures about a panda who speaks Chinese. Surely there must be a better way to get health insurance to cover his chronic congenital dermatitis... **216 pages $14**

COMING SOON

"Ballad of a Slow Poisoner" by Andrew Goldfarb

"House of Houses" by Kevin Donihe

"Ultra Fuckers" by Carlton Mellick III

"Super Cell Anemia" by Duncan Barlow

"Wall of Kiss" by Gina Ranalli

"Cocoon Of Terror" by Jason Earls

"HELP! A Bear is Eating Me!" by Mykle Hansen

ORDER FORM

TITLES	QTY	PRICE	TOTAL
	Shipping costs (see below)		
	TOTAL		

Please make checks and moneyorders payable to ROSE O'KEEFE / BIZARRO BOOKS in U.S. funds only. Please don't send bad checks! Allow 2-6 weeks for delivery. International orders may take longer. If you'd like to pay online via PAYPAL.COM, send payments to publisher@eraserheadpress.com.

SHIPPING: US ORDERS - $2 for the first book, $1 for each additional book. For priority shipping, add an additional $4. INT'L ORDERS - $5 for the first book, $3 for each additional book. Add an additional $5 per book for global priority shipping.

Send payment to:

BIZARRO BOOKS
C/O Rose O'Keefe
205 NE Bryant
Portland, OR 97211

Address		
City	State	Zip
Email	Phone	

Lightning Source UK Ltd.
Milton Keynes UK
19 January 2010

148755UK00001B/135/A